MISTRESS TO MURDER

Also by Robert Dietrich

The Steve Bentley Thrillers

Murder on the Rocks
End of a Stripper
The House on Q Street
Mistress to Murder
Murder on Her Mind
Angel Eyes
Calypso Caper
Curtains for a Lover
My Body
Guilty Knowledge

MISTRESS TO MURDER

ROBERT DIETRICH

CUTTING EDGE

ISBN-13: 978-1-952138-29-4

Published by
Cutting Edge Publishing
PO Box 8212
Calabasas, CA 91372
www.cuttingedgebooks.com

CHAPTER ONE

What I noticed first was the horse. It was ten yards off the bridle path, head down and nuzzling the young May grass. A handsome brown mare, flanks slick with sweat, saddled and with the bridle trailing through the early morning dew. A hard-ridden mount with no rider in sight.

Pulling to the side of the parkway, I stopped and let the Oldsmobile while I looked around. Turning off the engine, I got out, stepped over the low log railing that bordered the bridle path and walked toward the horse. Its ears pricked up and it eyed me. Beyond it were the rain-filled freshets of Rock Creek charging over the slate and pebble bottom toward the muddy Potomac. It was only a little after seven and the parkway was still free of Washington's morning traffic. Other than the rush of water there was no sound at all. As I walked toward the mare it moved warily away from me. I whistled and the mare stopped and lifted its head. It let me come close enough to grasp the bridle and lead it to a near-by pine. Making a hitch in the bridle I tethered the stray to a low branch and climbed a grassy rise toward the creek.

She was lying near the edge of the water, her arms outstretched, one knee drawn up. A girl in a chocolate suède jacket and doeskin jodhpurs. Her eyes were closed and her face was as white as a corpse.

Running to her, I knelt in the wet grass and listened to her heartbeat. It came in a slow relaxed rhythm. Still on my knees, I undid the top buttons of her suède jacket and felt gently behind her neck, lifting her shoulders to let the neck articulate. It moved with no grating of bones. Lowering her easily against the grass, I undid the rest of the jacket buttons and opened the coat. Then I began chafing her gloved wrists.

Her face was oval. A young face with high cheekbones, arching eyebrows and a small even nose. A beautiful face. Brown hair lay in a fan behind her head. Her hairline was scalloped by a widow's peak. High on the right side of her forehead was a blue-red bruise. Around her neck lay a fine gold chain. Against the open collar of her poplin shirt there was a small golden crucifix inlaid with tiny blue mosaic. The skin of her throat was white and the veins were close to the surface. I could see the pulse beating in the soft hollow of her throat like a tiny heart.

A flutter of her lips showed small even teeth the color of fresh ivory. She was breathing more deeply now, and as her bosom lifted and fell I could see that she was unusually nubile. Below her cheekbones her cheeks showed the attenuated concaves of undernourished fashion models, and even with her eyes closed her face held an elusive other-world look.

The chafing was getting us nowhere and her jodhpurs were soaking through with the morning dew. The bruise on her forehead suggested a concussion that ought to be X-rayed and so I got my arms under her shoulders and knees and lifted her. Carrying her toward my Olds was light and agreeable work. As I stepped over the low log railing I saw another car pulling over behind mine.

It was a big car. A long black Delahaye with a glass partition behind the driver's seat. The door opened and a chauffeur got out. He wore a gray whipcord uniform with brass buttons, a visored cap and black gloves. Jogging toward us he shouted, "What's the matter?"

"She's unconscious."

"How'd it happen?"

"Ask the horse. I wasn't around."

The chauffeur stopped and eyed me. He was over six feet tall and solidly built. From his face he looked a weather-beaten thirty and he hadn't bothered to shave. It was an angular face that looked as if it had seen its share of trouble. The lower part of the chin jutted outward making a recess at the base. He took off his cap as though it were too tight for him, scratched jet-black hair and put the cap slowly back on. "I'll take her," he said finally. "Thanks, buddy."

"Take her where?"

The eyes narrowed. "You looking for trouble, buddy?"

"I might be," I said. "Then again I might be simply looking after the young lady's welfare." I felt her right arm tense and move against me. Her body tightened then went slack. I glanced at her face but her eyes remained closed. Her eyelashes were so long they looked artificial.

I was still heading for the Olds. The chauffeur got in step and when I had laid her along the seat he said, "I told you I'd take care of her."

"She belong to you?"

Under the dark stubble his face flushed. "I work for the family," he grated.

"What family?"

"Any of your business?"

"Look," I said, "the girl's had a nasty fall. She's unconscious and there may be broken bones. She ought to be taken to a hospital with the less moving the better. I'll drive on down to Emergency and you can follow."

He moved toward me and stopped, his head cocked to one side. "You've done your Boy Scout bit for the day, buddy. Don't get over-interested in what ain't your property."

"Or what?" I said. "You'll take off the monkey suit and make me sorry?"

"Could be," he said easily, and I saw his shoulders shift. His gloved right hand balled into a fist and smacked into the palm of his left hand. "Like that."

"My, my. You've got me all chills and fever. You and your midnight TV dialogue. If you want to earn your pay there's

Dobbin over yonder needing a lump of sugar and a friendly word. Meanwhile, the young lady's riding with me. Eat it any way you want."

His half-closed eyes looked thoughtful. "What's your name?"

"Bentley. How about yours?"

"There's better ways of remembering people than names," he jeered. His right shoulder dropped and before I could move, a gloved fist was slamming into my face. I managed to get my jaw out of the way and the knuckles scraped along my cheekbone. I had a left to his belly ready but I never got a chance to use it. Out of nowhere his left fist came up and exploded on the point of my jaw. I had a brief spinning image of blue sky and pine branches as I went backward and then for a while a black curtain cut off everything.

The roar of a powerful engine brought me back. Opening my eyes, I raised myself onto one elbow and watched the Delahaye veer past my Olds and spurt down the parkway. My right finger traced the license number in the gravel.

It seemed a good place to rest, cool and reasonably comfortable. For a while I rested. The brown mare grazed and kept a scornful eye on me. Above, a robin flitted from branch to branch, chirped and flew off toward the water for a drink. A drink was what I needed. Something to ease the pain in my face. My right hand moved my jaw. Painful but not broken. Taken by a sucker punch, I thought disgustedly, with all the warning in the world. I pulled myself up groggily. shook myself and stared at the Olds. It was empty of course. The heavyweight in the monkey suit had her now, driving her God knows where. For me it had been a trip to the Fair with a record for brevity. As I staggered toward my car a powder-blue MG bore down the parkway and screeched to a stop behind the Olds. Behind the wheel sat a delicate young man in a bowler hat. Angled across the vacant bucket seat lay a furled umbrella. The driver peered at me and piped, "Anything wrong?"

"It's my own fault," I croaked. "I was trying out my new roller skates. At my age, too."

His eyebrows lifted. One long forefinger tapped against an upper incisor. "I don't see any skates but I do see a horse."

I turned and glanced back at the beast that had caused it all. "Very perceptive," I said. "But the nag had nothing to do with it. She just came along for horse laughs."

"Humph," the young man uttered in a displeased voice. "Some people aren't very appreciative when a person wants to be helpful."

"All too true," I agreed. "And it's probably a matter of breeding. I hope you don't meet anyone else as coarse as me the rest of the week."

"So do I," he said primly, pulled around my car with a growl of gears and shot down the parkway in a haze of blue smoke. I had an idea in the parking lot of which government agency his MG might be found parked, but delicacy forbade my mentioning the name aloud.

The brown mare was still grazing beyond the bridle path. Let Monkey Suit get her back to the stable. I slid behind the wheel and closed the door. Then I opened the glove compartment and pulled out a pint of scotch. It had been worked on previously but there was still enough left for what I wanted. I took two long pulls on the bottle and put it away. Cold out of the bottle the liquor tasted like cast iron. I blinked, felt my jaw and cheekbone and started the engine. The scotch in my guts was glowing charcoal, warming me and sending out little tendrils of wellbeing along my nerve-ends. Drinking seemed like a poor way to start a busy day but brawling was equally bad. Anyway, no clients were expected until ten o'clock. By then coffee would have cut the whisky breath and I would have a plausible story to account for my bruises.

None of that meant I had lost interest in the unconscious young lady and her strong-arm chauffeur. Before I pulled away from the curb I wrote the Delahaye license number on my note pad. It ought to be easy to trace: there probably weren't more than three or four Delahayes in the District; fewer of them chauffeur-driven.

I stayed on the parkway as far as K Street, turned east around Washington Circle and pulled onto Pennsylvania. The White House looked gaunt and lonely. The gates were closed and the guards were in their white guard-boxes, resting before the tourist queues formed for the ten o'clock opening.

At the garage I turned the Olds over to a sleepy attendant, walked back to the Washington Building and rode the elevator up to my office. Opening the blinds I looked down at the dirty gray side of the Treasury Building where I had put in several years before opening my own CPA office. I had friends there still punching the time clock, but they had families and couldn't gamble on making the break as I had. And Korea had helped.

My desk clock showed seven-thirty. That gave me an hour and a half to work undisturbed before Mrs. Bross reported in with her prim smile and her spinster's apprehension of everything outside the day's normal routine. But in a town as sparse of competent secretarial help as Washington I was lucky. Except for her hopeful annual vacation trips to Old Point Comfort, Mrs. Bross had been with me since the day my name had been lettered on the door. Other sexy little baggages had applied for the job but they had games or marriage in mind where I had a living to make. Thus, Mrs. Bross.

As I opened my files I thought back to my two years in Korea with the CIC: crooked PX and finance officers, the black marketers I had investigated and put behind bars. It seemed like a long time ago and it was. Too long ago. None of those men were in Leavenworth for life. While they were serving time they would remember who had put them there. And when the prison doors opened they would be bearing it well in mind. For that I had a shoulder holster and a Walther and a license to wear it.

The problem at hand was setting up two trusts to protect the estate and the business of a client for his son who would inherit it. I had had Hod Gurney draw a new will making the son co-trustee of the estate with exclusive right to vote the stock, recommended additional life insurance to maintain liquidity and otherwise done what I was being paid to do. I had a law degree from George Washington University but the town was filled with lawyers. What law I remembered helped in my tax practice but I always called in Hod to make the legal angles airtight.

By the time Mrs. Bross arrived I had drafted the final papers and put them in my Out box. As she lifted them, she scanned me with sharp eyes and said, "You look a little the worse for wear this morning, Mr. Bentley."

"I fell down in the shower," I ventured.

"Since when do you use an open-air shower? There's dirt on the side of your head. Not to mention your shoulders." She dusted the shoulders of my coat and said archly, "Or did you trip and fall in a winery, Mr. Bentley? That's how your breath smells, I'm sorry to say."

"I forget just how it happened. Anyway, I'm back all in one piece."

"Just barely," she observed and went into the outer office. I filled my pipe, lighted it and heard the comforting click of her typewriter. Everything was back to normal again.

Almost.

From my wallet I took the note pad with the Delahaye license number, stared at it thoughtfully and then I dialed the District Detective Agency.

While the phone was ringing I thought about the girl in the chocolate suède coat and the doeskin jodhpurs with the antique crucifix around her throat. A very choice morsel indeed and I could understand how anyone would want to regain custody of her in the shortest space possible. I wiggled my jaw again, remembering how it had been done. And by whom.

When the answering service cut in, I said, "I thought District never slept. Where the hell's Artie Von Amond?"

"The office opens at nine-thirty, sir. You may call then, or you may leave a message."

"That would be like writing Santa Claus," I said. "Garble, garble, garble. No thanks. I'll call later."

Hanging up, I left the office and went down to the Rexall for coffee and toasted muffins. The morning rush was over so I had a booth to myself and read the morning paper over a second cup of coffee. More atomic tests, more Soviet threats and more trouble in Africa and the Arab lands. Why bother to set up trusts and save tax money for clients when the world was going to hell in a red wagon? Under the circumstances any long-range projects seemed a waste of time.

Paying my check to the blond cashieress I picked up a box of Sen-Sen from the candy rack and her eyebrows lifted. "Hard night, Steve?" she asked coyly.

"It was nothing compared to the morning, sweetheart."

"I guess a hard-working guy like you has to take it out on something."

"There must be better ways." I dropped a quarter in the Community Chest box and eased out onto the street.

Back in my office I was about to ring Artie again when a call came from a distraught client whose bank account had just been frozen by the Director of Internal Revenue. I reminded him that I had advised him to pay his taxes on schedule and gave him an appointment for mid-afternoon. By then my ten o'clock client was waiting. At lunch time we moved the conference over to the Occidental for double spring lamb chops, musty ale and assorted hard stuff. He bowed out just as my garnisheed client arrived, and by four o'clock I had worked out his problem and was on my way to 12th Street and the Federal Tax Court for a hearing.

At six-thirty I stumbled out of the walnut doors, a favorable decision in hand, and caught a cab back to the office. When I had filed the papers and notified an overjoyed client, I remembered Artie Von Amond and called his office again. This time I was too late. Call tomorrow morning, the answering service girl enjoined me.

By seven-fifteen I was driving out Connecticut Avenue through thinning traffic, half-scanning it for a big black Delahaye with a girl passenger who looked like Pier Angeli. But nothing came of it. At Arbaugh's I treated myself to a double order of ribs and as many highballs and cut over to Massachusetts and out to my apartment. Collecting my key and accumulated mail at the desk I took the elevator up, loosening my tie on the way.

The mail was anything but interesting: fourth-class campaigns in behalf of poultry breeding, rat extermination and puzzle contests with a real American bike the ultimate prize. I crumpled it together in a wad and slammed it toward a waste basket. Then I pulled off my tie and began going through my pockets. Wallet, comb, ball pen, note pad, checkbook, parking stub ... and something else. Drawing it slowly out of my left-hand pocket I held it to the light.

A fine gold chain, broken, but still threaded through the link of a gold crucifix inlaid in microscopic blue mosaic. I laid it carefully on the table under the lamplight and stared at it. It couldn't have gotten into my pocket by accident. She had put it there. I remembered the unexplained movement of her arm after the chauffeur had called out to me, the tensing of her body. That had been when she broke the little chain and dropped it into my pocket.

Why?

A signal, obviously. A sign I was meant to understand. By then she was only feigning unconsciousness. She could have spoken to me but she hadn't. There was a reason for that, too. The same reason that explained the broken chain and the crucifix in my pocket. She was afraid to talk to me in front of Monkey Suit.

But what she had done silently and stealthily spoke more eloquently than fifty words. The girl was frightened and afraid.

Lighting a cigarette, I built a short highball and turned out the table lamp. A little more tenacity with Artie and by now I would at least have known who she was. I sat in the darkness thinking the whole thing over until my cigarette was dead and my glass empty. Then I pulled myself out of the chair and went groggily off to bed.

CHAPTER TWO

At six-thirty I got up, shaved while the coffee was perking and drove down the parkway along the Rock Creek bridle path. Parking where I had stopped the day before I filled my pipe, turned on the radio and waited. Yesterday's brown mare was gone, so someone had claimed her. A few early morning riders cantered past but none of them was the one I hoped to see. I waited until nearly eight and then I turned off the radio and drove the rest of the way to my office.

From there I called Artie Von Amond's house. His voice had a sleepy burr and when he heard mine he howled, "What the hell is it this time? Mention a corpse and I'll hang up."

"Hold on," I soothed, "I tried calling you yesterday but you were a little too spry for me. Then I got involved in other things—"

"I wish you'd stayed that way."

"—and thought I'd better get you where I was sure you'd be. In bed."

"You talk like I got no business in bed," he complained.

"Beds give you half your business, Artie."

"The wrong ones do. Not this one." I heard a thump as his fist hit the mattress. "All right, what is it?"

"Ten minutes' work. A license number—"

"Wait... Okay, I got a pencil."

I gave him the number slowly, repeated it and said, "A black Delahaye, chauffeur-driven. If you can get the name of the chauffeur, so much the better."

"What's he done?" Artie asked.

"Yesterday morning he cold-calked me."

"Why?"

"There was a girl, and—"

"I mighta known. Want the doll shadowed?"

"Not yet. But if her name pops up, write it down for me. Right now I'll settle for an address and the owner's name."

"You be at your office later?"

"I'm there now."

"You got no damn pity," Artie groaned. The receiver slammed down and the line went dead.

I hadn't planned on early morning work, but if Artie came through with what I wanted I would be out of the office at least part of the day. In my mind I could see the girl lying where she had been thrown. Again I saw the Delahaye stop and the chauffeur get out. Whose car was it? Her father's? Her husband's? Her hands had been gloved, hiding the absence or presence of a ring. In any case she was too young to have been married long. Her body was slim and lithe, her face calm and innocent; the face of a girl in her early teens. Except for the unusually developed bosom.

I thought of the hoodlum chauffeur lifting her out of the Olds and carrying her to the Delahaye, laying her down inside, even pawing her ... but before anything like that happened she would have let him know she was conscious. Or was it the frayed old story of the damsel and the driver ... ?

Until I heard from Artie there was nothing to be done. Perhaps not even then. Only if he came up with a name and an address. Because I wanted to see her again. Erect and with her eyes open. Anyone would. And I wanted to hear the sound of her voice. I wanted to learn why she had slipped the little talisman into my pocket, why she was afraid, who she feared. I wanted all those things. What I had was a file full of unfinished work. From it I culled enough for the next couple of hours, dragged the calculator into position and got busy.

When there was no call from Artie by ten, I called his office and his secretary said he was out. No message for me. Thanks a bunch, honey. Remind me to send you a week-old nosegay.

At ten-thirty Artie called. I knew from his voice he hadn't made out. "Not listed with the Automobile Club," he said.

"You wasted a dime to tell me that?"

"Sure. Steve, I got other clients, too. I'm on my way to the District Building now to check the registration lists."

"Hell, you should have started there."

"Little edgy, ain't you, boy?"

"From the fists I've been eating."

"Sure it was a District plate? You were woozy, remember. Couldn't be Maryland or Virginia?"

"Not unless the colors have changed."

"Okay, okay. No harm asking."

"Call when you get something."

Replacing the receiver, I shoved aside the pile of papers in front of me, lighted a cigarette and went out of the office. In the men's room I washed my hands and face and saw that the bruise on my cheek was on the way out. And the mark on the underside of my jaw couldn't be seen from a normal angle. That was something.

Six cigarettes later Artie called. "Got it," he said gleefully. "Better write it down. It's a foreign name. E-s-q-u-i-v-e-l. Esquivel. He's a Baron. Baron Alejandro Esquivel. Ever hear of him?"

"No."

"Me either. Buggy's a Delahaye, all right; black like you said."

"How old's the Baron?"

"Sixty-one."

"Good."

"Huh?"

"How about the chauffeur?"

"We're lucky on that. The Baron doesn't drive so we find the car is authorized to be driven by one Alfred Wells, age thirty. Same address as the Baron: up on R Street where the gentry live." He gave me the house number and I jotted it down. That placed the house near the northern limit of Old Georgetown. None of your reconditioned slave quarters there. Solid, old-time manses with plenty of trees and lawn and memories of hitching posts and carriage houses and the rest that went with gracious Southern living.

Artie broke in. "That all, Steve?"

"All for now. Many thanks, Artie. As always."

"Hope it does you some good."

"That's the last thing it'll do me," I said, but the line was dead. I couldn't blame him for being on the curt side after the way I'd pressured him. Beyond being an honest and reliable detective in a town filled with grifters and creeps, Artie was a friend. Time and again he'd laid his license on the line for me without my even having to ask. I'd been edgy all right. Working too hard. The income-tax rush was just over and while it was on I'd stayed at the office night and day: I needed a vacation. But there was no one around to suggest it to me or buy the tickets and shove me on the plane. No one except Mrs. Bross, and work to her was milk and honey. A no-nonsense lady. Well, wasn't that what I wanted? Hadn't I made her that way? Molded her in what I thought was my own image? And what did the image turn out to be but old Mr. Coffee Nerves himself. Not much satisfaction there.

Getting out of my chair, I switched off the desk lamp, got into my coat and walked out of the office. As I passed her desk Mrs. Bross looked up. "Early lunch?"

"Possibly."

Her forehead furrowed and her hands dropped into her lap. "Mr. Bentley, I hope you're not getting involved in another one of those things that always starts with calls from Mr. Von Amond."

"I hope not, too. Believe me, there's nothing I want less."

She looked at me severely. "When we started this business I knew everything about it. Until there was that big emerald you found, and then the business with General Ballou and his pretty daughter and…"

"You don't have to tick them off," I said. "I think of them often enough as it is."

"Well, at least I've had my say."

I opened my mouth to reply but her hands were on the keys again, clattering away like a tame machine gun. I walked on past her and took the elevator to the street.

For May it was a warm day. My ketch was scraped, varnished and painted and in the water off Maine Avenue. If the weekend weather was half as good it meant a long sail down the Potomac into Chesapeake Bay and back.

But first there was the matter of Baron Alejandro Esquivel and his gray-uniformed chauffeur. And the girl who was probably his daughter. As I got into my car I wondered how you addressed a baby Baroness.

When I reached R Street, Western High had just let out for the lunch hour. A group of kids playing stick hockey worked their way over toward Wisconsin and its beaneries. Others sauntered along arm-in-arm, soaking in the warm sunlight, enjoying the first of Washington's two livable seasons, the second being fall. The rest of the year was misery.

Turning east I saw the street number on an old brick postern gate. I parked and walked across the street to the iron gate that barred the drive. From where I stood I could see a wide stable that had been converted into a three-car garage. The stalls were empty, meaning that Al Wells and the Delahaye were away for the moment.

I rang the bell.

The fence around the big lawn was made of spaced brick posts with tall iron pickets between. Inside, rose bushes and a thicket of barberry backed up the fence to discourage anyone brave enough to climb over the iron spikes. Beyond, I could see stone benches and weathered statuary and two fountains and a group of cast-iron stags dispersed between the gravel walks and tulip beds. For May the grass was lush and the dogwood well along. The gardening alone would be full-time work for an able man.

Centered in all of this was the house. A big Victorian manse built of clapboard and painted slate gray. Flowers and ivy crawled upward along tall trellises toward scrolled gables and gingerbread turrets surmounted with lightning rods and weather vanes. The main turret was girdled by a Captain's Walk. It was the old Falconer place, the one-time abode of two eccentric spinster sisters who maintained the house and grounds in Victorian tradition until their deaths a few years back. If the interior had not been changed, it would offer plenty of ormolu, gilt sconces, whatnots, red-plush sofas and stereopticon viewers to the teatime caller. Just the land the old manse occupied was worth a sizable fortune, and it would take a couple of servants just to keep the dust moving from room to room. What little I had seen of the girl suggested anything but life in this Old Curiosity house.

No doors opened, no one came out of the house to open the gate. I leaned on the bell button again. By the time I had counted to ninety a side door opened and a female came out. She was wearing a black servant's uniform with more starched linen than a Brittany nun. As she hurried down the walk she pulled a long key from her apron pocket and clenched it in her hand. Slowing, she came up to the gate and gazed hostilely at me. I said, "I thought the bell might be dead."

"It wasn't." She was a dry, pinched woman with white wrinkled skin that looked as if it might see sunlight once or twice a year. By sheer chance.

She made no move to open the gate.

I said, "I came to inquire after the young lady who was thrown from her horse yesterday morning. I found her," I added brightly.

Her eyes squinted in the sunlight. "She's well enough."

"That cheers me," I said. "Now if you'll open the gate I'd like to pay my respects to her in person."

"Who might you be?" the pursed lips said.

"The one who found her. Remember."

The thin head moved slowly from side to side. "Wells said he found Miss Megan. Anyway he brung her back."

"That relieves me, too," I said. "Actually Al found her after I found her. If you get what I mean. Or is this all getting overly complicated?"

"Your name, young man?"

"You win." I took out my wallet and handed her a card. One without an adding machine in the corner.

She stared at it, making up her mind. Then she said sharply, "I'll have to ask the Baroness."

"By all means. I should have phoned. But then I don't have occasion to deal with royalty very often."

"There's them that's lucky," she rasped, pivoted and walked back toward the house.

I turned and leaned my shoulders against the postern. What short experience I had of the house suggested a long wait ahead. Lighting a cigarette I inhaled and loosened my collar slightly. The midday sun was burning away the air's normal stifling humidity, leaving it reasonably breathable. For 200-odd years Georgetowners hadn't been called residents; they were known as survivors. And the higher on Oak Hill you lived, the farther above the river, the better your chance to survive. After generations of periwigged Colonial snobbery, Georgetown began to disintegrate during the Civil War and kept declining until the New Deal's burgeoning horde of bureaucrats claimed it as their own. Then all through the Roosevelt Era the great renovation took place, turning rat-ridden, roach-infested hovels into quaint Federalist salons and collectors' traps. The gay folk fluttered in, too, with tiny art studios along Wisconsin, antique stores and chi-chi handmade-jewelry shops. For Georgetown is old town, new town, light town, dark town, queer town, quean town; and, with the exception of Foxhall Road, the most expensive collection of real estate in the nation's capital.

As for Washington it has, per capita, more rape, more incest, more illegitimacy, more perversion and crimes of violence than any city in the Western world. Along with that, more hotels and apartments, more politicians, more liquor, more seafood and gold toothpicks. All you need to survive is durability, money and powerful friends. And the more money the better.

I heard the scrape of shoes on gravel and turned around. The maid was coming back. No indication of the decision on her spare lips. Putting my hands around two gate bars, I hung back and smiled cunningly. "Faith, and it's glad I am to see ye again, Bridget."

Her eyes opened wide. "Name's Molly." Her face grew cautious. "Ye be from the green island?"

"Where else?"

Fitting the big key into the gate lock, she snorted, "If your name don't show it your big map does. Sure, an' I should of known. You're that handsome." Pulling open the gate, she tossed a glance over her shoulder toward the house. "Quare folk there, for the likes of me."

"Does Miss Megan like living here?"

Molly shook her head. "Poor thing, she's frightened half to death."

I stepped through the opening and Molly shut the gate behind me. When she had locked it we walked toward the house.

"From Megan she'd be a Gael, Molly."

"She'd be that—on her mother's side. Her father was a Spaniard. Dos Santos by name."

"What relation is the Baron?"

Her eyebrows lifted and her eyes searched the sky. "The Baroness be her half-sister. Or so they say. The Baroness is to talk with ye first, Mr. Steven. She'll decide if you're to see Miss Megan. Been in her bed since yesterday, poor creature."

"How old is Miss Megan?"

"Only nineteen."

At the front walk Molly turned left for the side entrance. I walked beside the porch until I reached the railed steps and went up, keeping my eyes on the door. As I walked I had the feeling that one of the curtains might have moved a fraction of an inch.

The upper half of the door was leaded glass, the little hexagonal panes gleaming like burnished silver. I searched the door frame for a bell or even a pull-cord, but there was nothing. Not even a knocker. Either you were expected or there was no point in coming.

In as much time as it took Molly to enter the side door and come through the house, she opened the front door and showed me into a card room off the main hall. I sat down in a fringed plush chair and surveyed my surroundings.

There was a round marble-topped table centered on an oriental rug. The long drapes were dark green velour. Against the patterned wallpaper an antique DeCock clock set in chiseled bronze with rose and cupid designs. Gilt sconces and a corner whatnot finished the furnishings. The whatnot held a collection of porcelain that looked as expensive as it was old: Meissen figurines, Capo di Monte seashells, a Bow tureen enameled with partridge and sheaf design, Sèvres and St. Cloud teacups. Overhead hung a crystal chandelier that needed polishing. It would always need polishing.

The air was as stuffy and still as an undertaker's anteroom. It lacked only the clinging scent of formaldehyde.

On the way in I had tightened my collar but I was ready to loosen it again just to breathe. And because the old Baroness might turn out to be a trifle overpowering, I wanted a cigarette and a double scotch, but there were no ash trays in sight and the place looked as if it would fall apart if anything stronger than sherry were uncovered before five o'clock.

Footsteps in the hall. I stood up to greet the chatelaine. The drapes parted and a lady came toward me, hand outstretched in a patrician welcome. I saw a woman of not more than thirty with short ash-blond hair, wide brown eyebrows and full lips. In her left hand an ebony cigarette holder with a lighted cigarette. She wore leg-tight loungies of gold thread brocade and a coral silk blouse, cut in a low center V and drawn tight around large high breasts.

As I took the outstretched hand she said, "How do you do, Mr. Bentley. I am Anita Esquivel."

CHAPTER THREE

I must have been gaping because she smiled in a reproving way and said, "Shall we go into the other room? We'll be more comfortable there."

Nodding I followed as she turned and led the way across the hall into the living room. Her voice had been faintly accented, the measured pronunciation British, as though her English had been learned somewhere on the Continent. In her face was something of the elfin beauty of her half-sister, but this was a mature self-assured woman. Her eyes were as gray as steel and she walked in a postured sensual rhythm suggesting a ballroom entrance.

The living room was a larger model of what I had just left. Another larger chandelier, more period furniture, a thicker oriental rug and a grained marble fireplace with Empire andirons. The room was as dark as a mushroom cave. As she seated herself on the sofa her eyes were shadowed. She beckoned me to a place beside her and I sat down. "You may smoke if you like, Mr. Bentley."

I shook out a cigarette and lighted it. In the dimness the lighter flame flared like a torch and as she watched me her eyes were amused.

Exhaling, she lowered the cigarette holder and said, "It seems we have much to thank you for. When the maid brought your card I took the precaution of discussing the matter with my sister. She now recalls someone aiding her before the chauffeur came along."

"Precaution, Baroness?"

She smiled faintly. “We live quietly here, Mr. Bentley. Even obscurely, one might say. From time to time the Press tries to interview my husband—resorting sometimes to the most incredible pretexts. Because of the pearls, you know.”

I lifted my eyebrows politely.

“Golden pearls, Mr. Bentley. Among connoisseurs they have a certain fame. There are thirty-two of them, matched and graduated. There are other golden pearls in the world, of course, but because of the selection this string is unique.”

“Frankly, I didn’t know pearls came in gold.”

She laughed lightly. “These are from Venezuela—Maracaibo Bay—where the oil-laden waters give them their golden tint.” She raised her ebony holder to dismiss the subject. “But since you are not of the Press the pearls would not interest you. You came to inquire after Megan’s well-being and I am happy to say that she is resting comfortably after a quite unpleasant experience. Who knows how long she might have lain there had you not happened along?”

“She’d have been found by the chauffeur. He was following, after all.”

She nodded. “Wells let her get too far ahead. The bridle path twists through the woods and is not always visible from the parkway. It was partly his fault, but really Megan’s for jumping the stream with such a poor mount.” Her eyes met mine. “Sometimes I believe the child is determined to kill herself.”

“A Ferrari or a spirited horse,” I said. “Take your choice.”

She shook her head slowly, a little sadly. “We have not spoiled Megan, she’s not that sort at all. But of course you’ve never talked with her and that’s really why you’re here.” Her eyes seemed to narrow suddenly I said nothing. She uncrossed her legs and sat forward. They were long legs, beautifully tapered from the thighs. Under the tight brocade I could see calves muscled lightly as a dancer’s.

Her voice dropped half an octave and said thoughtfully, "You *did* come here about Megan, Mr. Bentley?"

"Yes."

"No other reason?"

"Can you think of one?"

She shrugged. "I might—if I were not so curious over how you learned where Megan lived. She could not have told you because she was unconscious." Her eyes lifted and her head tilted slightly. "Or was she?"

"She was."

"Then how . . . ?" The question trailed away like a wisp of smoke.

I said, "Why make a mystery of it, Baroness? The chauffeur—Wells, you say—came along as you know. Couldn't Wells have told me?"

Her head moved slowly, negatively. "I don't think so, Mr. Bentley. You see, Wells never mentioned you at all. Neither did Megan—until a few moments ago. And even then rather vaguely."

"Why wouldn't Wells have told me?"

"Because he is hired to protect us from inquisitive people. So I am sure that it was not Wells who told you. You must have gone to a great deal of trouble to find Megan. I wonder why, Mr. Bentley?"

"Skipping over your doubts, Baroness, I found this crucifix in the grass and wanted to return it." From my pocket I pulled out the chain and the little crucifix. "It looked expensive and old. I thought the girl might like to have it back."

She studied it in my palm but made no effort to claim it. "It is both old and expensive. Twelfth century, I believe. But why could you not have given it to Wells?"

Sitting forward I lifted my chin and pointed to the dark bruise. Her eyes became vaguely interested. Nothing more.

Suddenly she stood up, placed one hand on her hip and said, "A drink, Mr. Bentley."

"Nothing heavy. A light scotch, maybe. For the dust."

She walked noiselessly to a tasseled pull cord by a wall tapestry and yanked it twice. Then she came back and sat down beside me. Also soundlessly and with no detectable exertion. Stubbing out her cigarette she tucked the holder into a slash pocket and said, "All this fencing seems so pointless. It was good of you to help Megan and to go to the trouble of returning her crucifix. It belonged to our mother. If Alejandro were here he would have been more courteous than I. I am sorry he is not here."

"Are you?"

Her eyes narrowed. "What did you say, Mr. Bentley?"

"Are you really sorry your husband isn't here?"

"I'm afraid I …"

Just then Molly came in carrying a gadroon edged silver tray half as big as a polo field. It held a silver bucket of ice and all the right bottles. She lowered it to the marble-topped table in front of us and went away. I mixed two highballs and handed one to Baroness Esquivel. Her eyes had never left me. Her tongue flicked tentatively into the glass and then she tilted it and drank a solid jolt. I did the same. We put down our glasses together and stared at each other. Finally I said, "All right. Wells didn't tell me anything. How I found out is my business. Okay?"

"O-kay." The word sounded awkward coming from her lips as it did in two distinct syllables. "Why did you ask what you did about my husband?"

I said, "The Baron's double your age, Baroness. I thought you might welcome a quiet drink with someone of your own generation."

The eyes and the lips formed a lynx smile. Slowly she said, "You may call me Anita. Actually I do. You knew it. But was it entirely gentlemanly to make me confess?"

"Probably not. But Cervantes laughed the old chivalry kick out of existence several hundred years ago. I don't know how long you've lived here or how many Americans you've known but we tend to get brutally frank on short acquaintance. For example, when I first saw you I was expecting a beefy dowager twice your age and with a Sig Ruman accent. That threw me off balance. Since then I haven't been responsible. So the fault's actually yours."

She laughed and reached for her glass. Lifting it, she touched it to mine. "I rather enjoy you, Mr. Bentley. . . ."

"Steve."

"Of course—Steve."

I tilted my glass and gulped enough for a thirsty gunnery sergeant. Then I glanced around the room. "A place like this would give me the fantods. For the Falconer sisters Victoria Regina was still in charge and Clive was whipping India into shape. But for you . . ." I let the thought trail away.

She surveyed me speculatively and finished her drink. I freshened both glasses and leaned back against the sofa. The scotch was as smooth as warm honey. If I felt much more comfortable I'd take off my shoes and prop both feet on the table. It was that kind of scotch.

She had lighted a cigarette. Exhaling, she leaned back and stretched, giving the silk blouse a hard test. Before anything gave she lowered her arms and kept looking up at the ceiling. In a detached voice she said, "How well you analyzed my situation."

"Exactly. You look the Cap d'Antibes type to me, but instead you're cooped up in the Garfield room at the Smithsonian with a constant battle against moths." I swallowed more of my drink and realized I'd neglected the soda. Two more like that and I could cross the ceiling on my hands.

Her head fell forward and her hand stuck the ebony holder between her lips. "The Baron collects firearms," she said. "Perhaps you'd like to see his collection."

I nodded and stood up. It was her play, her pace. She looked up at me wordlessly until I put out my arm to pull her to her feet. It could have been accidental but as she rose toward me she seemed to be coming too fast and we collided briefly. Just long enough to feel soft female flesh and sniff the light perfume of her hair. Her eyes widened, she clung to me as though to steady herself and then she moved away toward a sliding double door. Picking up both glasses I followed.

The room was the library. Built-in bookshelves laden with ancient tomes, a buffalo skin rug, a dark oak cabinet with more period porcelain and a gilded Louis Quinze escritoire near the single window. While I was looking around the Baroness closed the doors and went to a wall cabinet. Opening its doors, she pulled out a thin wooden tray, one of a number, and carried it to the desk. I worked on my drink while she opened the top of the tray.

The tray was a cloth-lined fitted case holding a pair of silver-chased flintlock pistols and accessories. I walked to her and handed her the highball. Then I lifted out one of the pistols and held it toward the light. It smelled faintly of oil. The grip was minutely checkered and the heavy octagonal barrel was as brown as burnished walnut. I pointed it toward the window, feeling the perfect balance, and she said quickly, "Do be careful. That one may be loaded. One of each pair always is."

"Which twin has the Toni?" I said. "And why?" The pistol's balance was a thing of beauty and precision. It was not meant to be aimed, but pointed like a long forefinger.

She shrugged. "It is how Alejandro keeps them. Perhaps for protection, perhaps for the sense of danger, however small. Do you shoot. Mr. Bentley?"

"Some."

"Under what circumstances?"

"When I have to," I said, still admiring the balance.

"The pistol is French, made by Boutet in 1791. It was a dueling pistol."

Putting it back in its lined recess, I shook my head. "Too ornate. Too much silver to distract a duelist's eye. And Boutet's name is engraved on the side. If it was a dueling pistol he'd have engraved his name on the top."

She looked chagrined.

"A set like this could have cost up to the equivalent of twenty thousand dollars in those times."

"I know." She closed the tray, put it back in the cabinet and brought back another tray. Opening the top she took out one of the pair and handed it to me. It was a saw-handled flintlock with a trigger-guard spur, heavy octagonal barrel and no ornamentation. On the top of the barrel near the breech hole I read the engraved name: *Jos. Manton 1818.* I finished my drink and examined the pistol. The flash pan was naked of powder. Pulling back the cock I dropped my arm, brought it up in a quadrant sweep and pulled the hair trigger. The cock snicked sharply against the flash pan, sparking the flint. I heard her exhale suddenly. "You frightened me. That pistol—or its mate—is the one that killed the Duke of Wellington. The set is the favorite of my husband."

Holding the heavy barrel in the crook of my arm, I said, "There's been a lot of nonsense written about dueling codes. The duelers didn't pace off the distance—seconds did. Aiming was illegal and there was only one round of fire. Powder charges were so small for the distances that only rotten luck was responsible for injury. Most of the ornate pistols sold as dueling pistols were really presentation pieces, never meant to be fired. Just a lot of gold, silver and platinum mounted on a handsome frame. To give the owner a sense of virility."

She took the pistol from me and replaced it. Turning, she murmured, "Are you applying that to Alejandro?"

"I don't even know your husband."

"But you suggested..."

"Nothing," I said. "You were the one who suggested it. But if he's only sixty-one there shouldn't be anything wrong with his performance. Unless he debauched in his youth."

Her gray eyes were veiled. She glided toward me and tilted her face upward. I put my arms around her and kissed the full lips. They were taut and warm. I found my fingers moving through her hair. Finally she moved away and said throatily, "That was a mistake. It should not happen again."

"It probably won't. Still it proved my theory."

The back of her hand covered her lips. "Was that why you did it? Only for that?"

I shrugged. "I had the idea you were expecting it—even suggesting it. I could have been wrong."

Her hand reached out and slapped my cheek lightly. For a rebuff it was the absolute minimum. And her eyes were dancing.

"Evil man. First you lie to me, and now this humiliation."

I nodded sadly. "Who knows where it might all end? Now that I've viewed your husband's treasures shall we go see baby sister?"

"If that is what you want."

While she put away the Manton flintlocks I lifted the empty glasses and carried them back to the tray. Most of the ice was melted but there was still enough scotch for a Kansas City Elks Convention. The old house had its compensations.

I heard the sliding doors close and then she had fitted one arm through mine and was drawing me toward the hall. At the doorway she paused long enough to yank the pull cord and then we were going upstairs, drifting in a scotch mist that made climbing effortless.

Above a long hall, carpeted with a thick red runner and hung with morose Dutch oils. Finally an oak door. As we stopped, she looked up at me and I kissed her again. It lasted longer this time and her body molded against mine as though it were plastic.

Nuzzling the feathery hair above her forehead, I said, "Why don't we stop this, Anita?"

"Animal," she hissed and bit the end of my tongue.

I dabbed away lipstick with my handkerchief and adjusted my tie. Then she opened the door and we went in.

It was a big corner room with more light than the rest of the house put together. The bed was a mahogany four-poster with a white tulle canopy above. Propped up by big overstuffed pillows lay the girl I had found yesterday morning. Over her bruise was a small bandage. Beside her lay a copy of *Doctor Zhivago.*

Anita said, "This is Mr. Bentley who found you, Megan. He brought back your crucifix."

The girl sat up, eyes wide. In her frilly bed jacket and without make-up she looked even younger than the day before. But no less nubile. Quietly she said, "Thank you so much, Mr. Bentley. You were very kind."

Walking toward her I brought out the crucifix and its severed chain and handed it to her. "I'm glad I found this."

"So am I." Her eyes held the half-hopeful half-hopeless expression of a wounded quail in the mouth of a retriever.

I said, "Having the chain repaired would have taken time and I wanted you to know it wasn't lost."

"I wouldn't have wanted you to trouble." Her speech was less accented than her sister's. The voice was softer and less assured. Her eyes were larger than I had imagined and hazel color. Glancing down at her hands, I saw that there were no rings on her tapering fingers. Well, hell, she was only nineteen.

From behind me Anita said, "You see, Mr. Bentley, Megan is quite well."

"It could have turned out differently." I looked down at her.

"The horse balked," Megan said. "I'll never ride her again."

There was the sound of a car on the gravel drive below. Her eyes darted upward to mine. "My guardian," she said. "And Wells, the chauffeur. Perhaps you remember him from yesterday."

"I'll never forget him."

Anita's voice was vexed. "I must greet Alejandro. Please come down soon, Mr. Bentley. We must not tire my sister."

Turning, I said, "I'll be right down." Clearly Anita didn't want to leave us alone. She went out, leaving the door open.

As her footsteps receded Megan lifted one finger to her lips. The other hand raised the heavy book and opened it. "Have you read this yet?"

"I tried."

She handed the open book to me. Pressed against the page lay a scrap of paper torn from the jacket. On it were printed five words. I read them, pocketed the scrap and nodded. She smiled uncertainly. "Do you find it hard to understand?"

"A little," I said. "But I suppose it ends like most novels—with a happy ending."

"I haven't read that far."

"It's an old formula. We might talk about it more another time."

"I would like that." She held out her hand and I took it. "Thank you again, Mr. Bentley."

"If I'm anything I'm dependable." From below came the sound of mingled footsteps. A door opened and closed. I walked away from the bed and through the open door. Something had constricted my throat but loosening my collar wouldn't help. It came from inside.

Down the carpeted stairs to the hall where a man and woman were talking. They stared up at me, Anita and the Baron, and I looked down at them.

He was a well-built man with wider than usual shoulders and skin that had barely begun to wrinkle. His gray hair was combed straight back from his high forehead and it curled around his ears. His eyes were sharp and piercing and his teeth had been capped. His chin sported a gray spade goatee. He looked ten years younger than his known sixty-one. The dark worsted suit he wore couldn't have cost less than two hundred dollars at going rates. The lapels were crisply pressed and sported a small white carnation. His coat was open enough to show a heavy gold chain across a fawn-colored waistcoat. Spats, a gold-topped cane and a crush fedora would have qualified him as a boulevardier. But there was little of the dandy about him. Even at that distance I could feel his presence. It pressed down on the house like heavy ice on a winter roof.

As I reached the floor Anita made the introduction. The Baron shook my hand with a grip like a miner. If I hadn't anticipated his strength I would have drawn back a hand as limp as a damp washcloth. He said, "Thank you for your help and interest, sir."

"I'm glad to find the patient is coming along."

Anita looked worriedly at him, but the Baron said, "My wife tells me you are interested in my pistols. Perhaps we could examine them together one day."

"With pleasure."

Then the shaking of hands again as I was eased toward the door. Molly was waiting to open it for me, her face blank as I said good by.

A very smooth article, the Baron. A very choice article, his wife. A nifty. Hell they could even be legitimate. Both of them. And upstairs a girl afraid to talk aloud in her own home. I went down the walk and saw Wells at the open gate waiting to lock it after me. As I neared him I saw a sneer form on his lips. A yard away I stopped. "Hello, Alfred," I said. "It didn't quite work, did it?"

"Holding a grudge? Take some advice, Bentley. Stay away, huh? Get lost."

"Tsk, tsk. And such a proper monkey. Why all the dirty mud on pretty boots, Alfred?"

As I had meant him to he glanced down just long enough to let me sink my left into his belly. He jackknifed with a loud grunt.

My right caught the side of his chin and he went down sideways. He was a tough baby with a lot of fight in him and he grabbed for my legs, but too late. My right knee rammed into his temple and he hit the gravel spread-eagled, his eyes staring up blankly, the visor cap spinning a yard away. I stared down at him for a moment and rasped, "Don't ever think I don't hold a grudge." Stepping over him, I walked out through the gate and across the street to my car.

As I got in I didn't look back at the house but I had the feeling I was being watched, and not by Alfred. I drove east and at the first stoplight I got out the note Megan had written and read it again. A short message. Just five words. As I held it my hand was shaking: *Montrose Park. Tonight. Nine o'clock.*

CHAPTER FOUR

Nobody had invited me to stay for lunch so I gnawed a sandwich at my desk and placed a call to Artie's office. It was a while before he called back and by then I had pretty much figured what I wanted to do.

I said, "My experience with the titled nobility is limited but I think we've got a cozy little vipers' nest up on R Street that might bear looking into."

"Yeah?" He sounded pleased. "How much looking?"

"Start on the Baron. Check Immigration to find when he came here and why. Where his visa was issued. He could be as legitimate as a government bond but there's always the negative chance."

"Okay."

"The Baroness is half his age. A trim little platinumed type and an easy nuzzler."

"Naughty boy."

"No special compliment to me. The hour of the day and the drinks. I doubt that she's love-starved because the spouse is a very well-preserved sixty. Either he's kind of an odd mixture or I don't dig the Continent. I don't know what business he's in, if any, but he seems to live pretty comfortably. An expensive collection of flintlock pistols and, according to his helpmate, a string of golden pearls worth slightly less than the Hope Diamond."

"Golden pearls?"

"From Venezuela. Nasty crude petroleum in the water gives them a special hue. You might ask Plum and Company or your insurance contacts for a rundown. If they're as special as the lady alleges the trade ought to know they're in town. She claims the Press is all sweated up about them."

"Will do. That all?"

"Not quite. To clear the air a little I took a quick decision from the chauffeur but I'm still curious about him. Big burly ape, not too bad-looking in a way that might just appeal to someone as highly refined as the Baroness. Knows how to swing a fist, too. Possibly there's something in police files on him."

"Alfred Wells, wasn't it?"

"I don't figure him as the Baron's type, but that would depend on just what type the Baron is."

"That's logical," Artie mocked. "Any other trivial data to add?"

"Nothing comes to mind."

He cleared his throat. "You could ask your buddy Kellaway to look into the police angle. He'd do it fast and for free."

"The hell he would. You know how snobbish they get down at Headquarters. A Homicide guy sneers at the dip and con squad. And Kellaway doesn't relish a corpse the way he used to. Another couple of years and he'll be on the White House detail for distinguished foreign visitors—striped pants and a white carnation. A P.D. bureaucrat."

Artie chuckled. "You told him that?"

"That's just taxicab dialogue."

"Well," Artie said, "how much time you giving me?"

"A lot. All the rest of the day."

Artie humphed. "What's in this for you, Steve?"

"That's what I keep asking myself."

"Same old Bentley," he said and hung up.

I replaced the receiver, stared at it for a while and went back to my drugstore sandwich: rye bread curled like the new moon and Swiss cheese with all the flavor of a wet plastic bag. The coffee was so light you could see the container bottom on a dark night.

Easily two entire beans had been used in making it. I belched sourly, shoved aside my lunch and began reviewing what work Mrs. Bross had finished in my absence. At one-thirty she came back and I gave her two tickets to the night's middleweight waltz at Uline Arena to send over to Artie. I had committed myself to something else: a meeting in Montrose Park with Megan Dos Santos. At nine o'clock. And I intended to be there.

A little after four Artie called, thanked me for the tickets and said, "Nothing from Immigration yet, you know how those system boys work."

"Slow, if at all."

"Yeah. But the jewelry trade knows all about the Maracaibo pearls. They're insured for a cool seventy grand and Plum says they'd buy them for that, cash on the line."

I whistled.

"The pearls were insured in Switzerland by a British combine less than a year ago. The Baron had to post a bond to bring them into the States because they're highly salable. The insurance date suggests the Baron hasn't been here very long. He's Spanish, by the way. Whether the title's legit or not I don't know. How the hell can you ever tell about a thing like that? I always figure half the titles are phony and the other half bastards."

"A passable rule of thumb. What else?"

"One of my bright young men called in to say this guy Wells holds a pistol permit. Only the name ain't quite the same. Welinsky it comes out. Date of issue seven months ago. The Baron was one of his references. The fliers weren't checked because the permit wouldn't have been issued if Welinsky had a record."

"Brief me on basics, Artie," I needled him. "Tell me about the Sullivan Law."

"Awright, awright."

"Got a couple guys for a tail job?"

"I can scrape them up. On who?"

"Welinsky."

"Hell, I figured the Baron. Starting when?"

"Tonight."

"Mobile?"

"Hell, yes, he's a chauffeur. Any chance you'll have the Immigration data tomorrow?"

"I got it flagged Rush. Satisfied?"

"Not too bad for a first go-round," I conceded.

"You sweet on the Baroness, by any chance?"

"Not if I'm in my right mind."

"That's what they call the big question, Stevie. You ain't always the most logical guy in town."

"Even my enemies credit me with conservative judgment, vision and dogged devotion."

"Says which?" he cracked and hung up.

I gnawed a jagged thumbnail and reviewed the bidding to date. I was three steps up a long and winding staircase but the Baron and his household remained as much of a mystery as yesterday. Grappling with Anita Esquivel had been light, agreeable duty but it hadn't revealed anything more than the obvious fact that she was playful—something I could have guessed from a distance. What little sister's problem was hadn't come out yet and nine o'clock was nearly five hours away. I could do a lot of speculating by then, but she was going to tell me all about it, so why bother.

Mrs. Bross came in with some forms to be signed, discussed a moot point with me and when she went out I got back to work again. At five-thirty she said goodnight and left me alone in the office. I was catching up on some professional reading when the door buzzer sounded. Probably the elevator man with a Special Delivery from an uneasy client.

I got up, walked through the outer office and opened the door.

Instead of an elevator operator in black whipcord the man who stood there wore a cream-colored gabardine raincoat and a matching rain hat. The gun was only a bulge in his right pocket but his hand was around the butt and I was willing to assume a finger around the trigger. He had hard eyes and a frosty smile on his lips. They parted like floe ice and said, "Bentley?"

"He's gone."

The gun in his pocket lifted slightly. "Who're you supposed to be?"

"Junior partner."

His tongue cluck-clucked. He rode me back inside the office and leaned on the door. "Easy," he told me. "Just ever so easy. The billfold. Don't drop it, don't slam it at me. Just toss it lightly. Get it?"

Slowly I pulled my coat open with my right hand and plucked out my wallet with my left. I tossed it toward his outstretched hand as gently as a toy balloon. He opened it, glanced at my driver's license and tossed the billfold back at me. I caught it and worried it out of sight. My throat was tense and dry. Baked sand was never so dry.

He smiled. Not much of a smile for such a big man, but a smile. If you could call it that. And I wanted to. I wanted something warm and friendly in a room that had suddenly grown as cold as an Antarctic hut. "Shame on you," he said, "carrying the boss's wallet. I heard Bentley was on the smart side. Letting you pick his pocket don't sound all that smart, now does it?"

"Little things upset me," I said. "Like having a stranger hold a gun on me. For a moment I forgot who I was."

"Swell," he said. "Real swell. I kind of figured you was Bentley all along."

"From the description?"

His eyebrows rose slightly. "Could be. Now, why do you suppose I'm here?"

"You've got the stage," I said in a voice as brittle as dry nettles. "I'll do the listening."

The eyes never left me. His free hand fished out a cigarette and lighted it. I found myself licking parched lips. Blowing smoke toward me, he said, "You got a nice little business here, friend. I hear you do all right for yourself. Work hard, stick to your own line and you got a nice comfortable future ahead of you."

"That sounds like good advice."

"Take it," he rasped suddenly. "Deal yourself out of the R Street house and stay away. Don't even kibitz."

I took a breath to steady myself. "I guess somebody doesn't love me," I croaked.

"I wouldn't even bother to guess who. There'd be too much to lose. Any questions?"

"If any occur to me where would I call for answers?"

He gave me a cracked smile, shifted his weight and said, "You as tough as you sound, Bentley?"

I spread my hands. "Me? I'm the kind of guy dogs love. Ask anyone."

He grunted, the gun barrel flicked upward another inch and he said, "I wouldn't have picked you for a humble gee, Bentley. Shows a fellow can be wrong. Once in a while. So far we get along great. Only I wouldn't like to have to come back. Kind of get the idea?"

"I've been two furlongs ahead of you," I said. "Now that we've had our chat I guess I owe you a vote of thanks for clearing things up, giving me new perspective."

His face wrinkled and his mouth went sour. "Nix," he grated, "the lines don't buy no laughs with me." He moved forward and I began to back away but it was only his hand turning the knob behind his back and pulling open the door. As he stood in the opening he said, "There's zero in this for you. So don't try tackling me in the hall or calling the cops or any other bright ideas. You want to be a hero, go join the paratroops. Forget what I look like and remember what I said. Got it all straight?"

"Like the Baltimore Turnpike." I watched the door close slowly on his tall figure. I stood there listening to his heel clicks recede down the hall and then I began to shiver. It was an old threadbare scene, me standing in front of a hood with a gun. As a scene it stank. I had played it so often there was no novelty left. Not even the shakes. I bolted the door and went back to my desk. In the center drawer lay a pint bottle of Dutch courage. The label said Teacher's Highland Cream but it was what I needed. I uncorked it and let three ounces slide down my throat without missing a breath. From the label it was scotch but my mouth was so numb it could have been Chanel Number Fifty.

When the shivering stopped I corked the bottle, put it carefully away and sat down. The hood was a new face with an out-of-town accent. A coal-town tocker. The face was the lightest possible olive, smooth skin and hard lips. I would remember the lips. Like a fissure in cast iron. There was a small flat scar just over the socket of his right eye, an old scar only a little lighter than the rest of his skin. For all I knew he was bald on top—the rain hat hid all but a little hair, and what showed had been the darkest possible brown. About six-feet-two and one-ninety-odd. A big hand that could palm an average gun like a water pistol. That and an Ivy League rain outfit.

Getting up I went over to the window and peered down through the blinds. If it was raining it was still only mist. People coming out of restaurants, walking to the movie houses. Over at the National Theatre a new play from Broadway with the original cast. The Trans-Lux was featuring a new Bardot lust vehicle. At Constitution Hall a heavyweight soprano front Vienna. The middleweight dancers at Uline: Jake Fortunato *vs* Slim Spokane. Fifteen rounds for a crack at the title belt next July. Culturally a mixed bag. Washington.

Turning away, I looked at my disordered desk and listened to the after-hours silence of the building. Even the hoods had gone. I felt alone and lonely, isolated from the scurrying ants on the street below: tired government girls, bachelor clerks; duck-tailed young men in Levis and black-leather jackets; hard-eyed dykes and mincing queans; sleek lobbyists; politicians; butter-and-egg men from out of town; hillbilly tourists of all shapes and ages; pimps, Congressmen, Senators and big wheel bureaucrats.

But away from the downtown streets, up in the big glassy apartment houses on Connecticut, were the hidden harems of the rich and powerful. Sleek, long-limbed blondes; fragile dark brunettes; hearty big-breasted redheads; underage Virginia quail, potential statutory rape cases. Paris clothing and mutation furs, champagne and scotch and delicately-scented liqueurs. Low imported sports cars and diamond brooches and sapphire clasps from Plum & Company, and rings. All but the right one.

I wanted to be in a low-lighted cocktail lounge playing handies with a fragile feather-cut blonde, listening to good piano and the tinkle of ice and the vibrant hum of women's voices. I wanted sounds and music and people. What I had was silence and strange thoughts.

I went out of the office and locked the door.

I drifted down to the Occidental and there was a crowd but not too big a crowd. A table for one, two double scotches and grilled mutton chops with a crisp mixed salad. Apple pie and French vanilla ice cream. *Espresso* and cognac and out into the night.

The air was cool and damp, the sky starless. Through scattered traffic I drove out Massachusetts. Embassy Row. Glittering cars, white gloves and ballroom gowns; candlelight and low conversation in a dozen languages. Ambassadors, Ministers, Counselors and Chargés d'Affaires a.i. Fine-boned, haughty women with sculptured faces and enameled receiving-line smiles. Jewel-bright eyes that saw all and told nothing. The world of diplomacy. Phony as a dime-store sparkler.

Parking in front of the apartment I locked the Olds and strolled the crescent walk to the door. At the desk the clerk gave me a superior smile. “No mail.”

I stepped back from the desk and looked around the lobby. The clerk’s eyes followed me worriedly. He coughed and said, “Expecting a visitor?”

“Only the courier from Damascus,” I said, “plus a couple of veiled women. When he comes tell him to bring the diplomatic pouch right up. The goats, too.”

“Goats?” he chirruped.

“Of course,” I said. “It’s their custom. A dairy where-ever they go. Be deferential about it, too.”

“Goats,” he squeaked again. “Why, the management would never—”

“Argue with State,” I snapped and left him twittering to the switchboard operator.

I fitted a stereo tape on the Ampex, set the preamp dials and filled my pipe. Lighting it, I sat down, stretched out and closed my eyes. Music filled the room, suspending reality until the tape had run out. I sat up, blinked, tapped away cold pipe ashes and stood up. I stretched, yawned, scratched my shoulder and massaged the kneecap that had connected with Al Welinsky’s temple. Then I took a shower, shaved and put on a clean shirt. A bow tie would take away five years so I put on a dark blue one of Siamese silk, buttoned down the collar points and pulled on a pair of flannel slacks. From the top of my closet I got my 9mm Walther and strapped on the shoulder holster. Pulling out the grip magazine, I counted the shells, checked the chamber and clicked the magazine back into place. I slid the pistol into the shoulder holster and got into a tweed coat. It wasn’t normal equipment for meeting a young lady of nineteen, but the evening hadn’t been entirely normal either. The gozzler in the cream raincoat had learned about me from somewhere; from someone in the old R Street museum. He could be watching Megan as well.

Cigarettes, pipe, tobacco, lighter. The tweedy up-country smell that women are reputed to crave but probably detest. Locking the apartment door I rode down to the street and piled into my Olds.

There was time to kill. I drove down Massachusetts past the big Gothic cathedral and turned onto Wisconsin. Shopping centers, beersteubels, second-run flics, hopeful little hat shops with economically lighted windows. Classical record stores, modistes, laundromats, chop suey dens. Then left past Dumbarton Oaks and finally the trees and fence of Montrose Park.

The gates were locked. At the corner of Lovers Lane a cop leaned against the lamppost, twirling his nightstick. A dark, heavy night with more than a premonition of rain. Pulling over to the curb, I dimmed my lights and let the engine idle.

I lighted a cigarette and let smoke drift out of the lowered window. My wrist watch showed nine o'clock. Craning I peered along the empty sidewalk. Even the patrolman had gone. I smoked and pondered Megan Dos Santos and her sister and the muscular Baron, and then there was a distant figure hurrying toward me out of the dimly lighted obscurity. As it passed a street light I saw a girl in a short gabardine raincoat, a stack of books under one arm. I blinked my lights and saw her lift one arm tentatively. She passed the nearest street light and I saw the brown-haired girl of the Pier Angeli face and the hazel eyes. She left the sidewalk and angled across the grass toward the curb. I opened the door and let it swing outward. She reached it breathlessly, paused to glance at my face and then she got in and closed the door.

"We can't stay here," she said tightly. "We'll have to go somewhere else. Please hurry."

I put the car in gear and pulled away from the curb. At Wisconsin I turned south, heading toward the river.

CHAPTER FIVE

Her books lay on the seat between us. She saw me glance at them and said, "I'm supposed to be at the library. I can't stay long."

"That's up to you."

She had turned away and was looking out of the window. Turning back, she said, "It was very kind of you to come, Mr. Bentley."

"I'm not too old to be called Steve," I said. "Anyway, I told you I was dependable. The air of mystery would have brought me if nothing else."

She put her hand near her throat and breathed deeply. "I guess I'm not used to running."

"You've had two days in bed."

She nodded.

"Smoke?" I asked.

"Well . . . yes."

I handed her the package and pointed to the dash lighter. "Don't they let you smoke?"

"Anita and Alejandro? They treat me as if I were a baby."

"There's something to be said for a careful bringing-up."

"Yes," she said bitterly, "there is, isn't there?" She lighted her cigarette and replaced the lighter. Turning to the window again, she watched the passing lights.

At K Street I turned east as far as the bridge and cut off onto the parkway. As far as the *Titanic* Memorial there were no other cars. I pulled around the circle, braked and cut off the engine and the lights. The river was a broad band of tarnished pewter, cold and sullen. Cars crawled across Memorial Bridge like beetles with orange eyes. Easing back in my corner, I lighted another cigarette. The flame showed her profile staring straight ahead. I said nothing. After a while her face turned slightly and she said, "What were you and Anita doing outside my door just before you came in?"

"Is that a proper question?"

"Perhaps not. But I have a right to know."

"Ask Anita."

Her face turned the rest of the way and I saw that her fists were clenched. "You were kissing her, weren't you?"

"What sharp ears you have, Miss Mouse."

"Don't call me that!" she stormed. "And don't be condescending because you think I'm a child. If you knew the way I've lived, what I've ..." Her fist raised to her mouth and I saw her teeth dent her knuckles as she fought back something close to hysteria.

"Suppose you tell me," I said quietly.

She shook her head, the hair fanning out briefly like a ballerina skirt. When the hand left her mouth her voice was calm again. "Anita is a woman of the world. Adult, sophisticated and beautiful. I can understand why men want her. All men. Only why do there have to be so many?"

I said nothing.

She leaned toward me. In an odd voice she said, "My sister is very experienced in love. I'm sure she knows how to thrill a man much better than I."

Her voice was so low that I had leaned toward her to hear. Her hands caught my lapels and drew me even closer. Then her face tilted upward, her eyes closed and her lips moved against mine. At first the touch was light and tentative. Then her mouth opened and her teeth nibbled the end of my tongue. Her breathing grew more rapid and when I put my arms around her I could feel the pounding of her heart. Then a shudder went through her body and she broke away. I looked at her and her eyes were moist. I said, "What do you want me to say, Megan?"

"That I'm…" She bit her lower lip. "That I can kiss as well as Anita," she finished bravely.

I put the cigarette between my teeth, inhaled and let the smoke drift upward. "Your sister and I really never covered that much ground. Besides you didn't really like it, so why go through the motions?"

"I did. I liked it a lot," she said defiantly.

I shook my head. "You're trying to convince yourself. You were scared, Megan. You felt something happening and you let go. You were frightened. I think you were ashamed of the way you felt. You're ashamed of your sister and so you've come to think that passion is shameful, even dirty."

Her eyes had grown large. Her lips trembled and she turned away. I said, "Kissing's fun—with the right person. But it isn't the end of the world. It goes on from there. And keeps going."

"As if I didn't know," she said thickly. "People are no better than animals."

"I won't argue it. Anyway, we didn't come here to debate sex—at least I didn't. You have a beautiful face, an extraordinarily provocative body and you know the elements of kissing. For nineteen that's a lot. Now let's take it back to yesterday morning when I found you. You weren't unconscious when I carried you to this car. You broke the crucifix's chain and slipped it in my pocket. You did it knowing I'd look for you. Well, I did, and I found you. About nine hours ago you contrived to give me a message to meet you tonight. Suppose we explore the reasons why. Are you in danger from anything or anyone?"

Her head dropped and her eyes fixed on her hands. After a while she stubbed out the cigarette and said, "Not in the way you mean. I hate Anita. I hate Alejandro. I can't stand them any longer."

"Why?"

Her face turned to mine and she said evenly, “Do you think I’m mad?”

“Everyone is—a little.”

She shrugged. “Don’t draw out things I don’t want to speak about, things no one must ever know. They watch me, they never let me out of their sight. I have no friends, no one who can help me. We’ve had scenes time after time, but they say they’re just solicitous of my welfare—they want me to grow up a lady.” Her lip curled. “A lady. When my sister is a high-class whore and Alejandro a thief.”

“What about Wells?”

“He tries to touch me. Tries to find moments when we’re alone. Once he tried to kiss me and I scratched his face. But still he watches me, still tries…” Her voice quavered and broke. She dabbed at her eyes with a small handkerchief. “I don’t want to talk about it anymore. I need help. Will you help me?”

“What is it you want?”

From her coat pocket she drew a slip of paper. “When we lived in Lisbon there was a maid who worked for us. She was my friend. Alejandro brought her here. Now she lives by herself.”

“Did he fire her?”

She laughed thinly. “He pensioned her to get her away from me. He pays her well but she is still loyal to me. Will you go to her and ask that she give you something she has kept for me?”

I took the slip of paper, snapped my lighter and looked at it: a name and an address, nothing more. Lucia Melho. An address on Garvin Street over beyond Union Station, South East.

Megan said, “Lucia knows enough English to understand you. Whatever she gives you, will you bring it to me tomorrow night?”

I nodded.

She glanced at the dash clock. “I must go back now. If I am not at the house soon they’ll begin looking for me.”

I started the engine, turned on the lights and pulled back onto the parkway. Megan was silent until I turned up Wisconsin and then she said, "No questions, Steve?"

"What about your father?"

Her lips tightened. "He and Alejandro were in business together in Spain. One day my father and mother were driving together along the coast near Irun. The car went off the road and crashed down into the sea. Something in the car had broken, they said later. After that Anita and I went to live with Alejandro."

"Your mother's first husband—Anita's father?"

"He was killed in the Civil War. At Burgos."

"Which side?"

She turned toward me. "What difference does it make now?"

"Is Alejandro—the Baron—legitimate?"

She smiled briefly. "In a sense—the title is an old one. Alejandro purchased it so now it is his."

"Where does his money come from?"

"My father was a banker. So was Alejandro. It was a business that went between Berne and Madrid."

"Legitimate?"

"Not entirely. They dealt in foreign exchange. Wealthy Spaniards keep their money any place but in Spain. They entrusted it to my father and Alejandro smuggled it to Switzerland and deposited it in secret bank accounts."

"A lot of money?"

She nodded slowly. "A great deal of money. These people trusted my father. They never knew Alejandro existed. Not until after my father was killed."

"Killed?"

"An expression. He died."

"What about the secret accounts?"

A thin smile crept over her mouth. "Only Alejandro knew which numbered account belonged to what person. After my father was dead Alejandro went to those people and offered to find their money—for a large fee, of course. Those people who refused never saw their money again. That is why he is a thief. That is why we came to America. Lisbon was too close to the Spanish frontier. A man wanting to kill Alejandro could cross the border find him in Lisbon and be back in Spain by nightfall. Here that would be more difficult to do." Her glance fell away. "This must sound very strange to you. America is different from Europe. Here things like that do not happen."

"Don't be too sure," I said. "Men are murdered here and the reasons are stocks and blondes and oil wells and slot machines. But the motive is usually the same: money."

"Greed," she echoed. "You know about the golden pearls?"

"Anita told me."

"Anita would. Alejandro said he bought the pearls for her. If she believes that she is a fool." Her mouth was bitter. "My sister deserves them. God, how she deserves them. Even bought with stolen money."

I said, "Are Anita and the Baron married?"

"They went through a ceremony in Portugal. Whether there is any proof…" She spread her hands. "I tell myself that they are man and wife."

"And what you want is—"

"To get out," she said harshly. "To leave them and their shabby deceits and their little cruelties and their rottenness. God, how much I want to leave."

I said, "You don't have to go back there tonight, Megan."

Turning she looked at me again. "One needs money to exist. I have nothing. Not even the money my father would have wanted me to have. When I go I will have money enough to last a long time."

We were nearly at the corner of R Street. I pulled over to the curb and stopped the car. Her hands lifted the books onto her lap. She leaned toward me and her lips brushed the side of my face. "Tomorrow night," she whispered. "The same time and place."

"Why should Lucia give me anything at all?"

"Tell her that my father's name was Raul and she will know that you are helping me. Will you see her very soon?"

"I can go there tonight."

"Thank you," she breathed, opened the door and got out.

I watched her shift the heavy books in her arms and begin the upward walk to R Street. She looked like a schoolgirl on her way from the library. Innocence and a core of toughness and her own view of the world.

As she turned the corner she glanced back and I wondered how much of what she had told me was true and how much dramatic imagination. When I had time I would sift it but the part I believed without question was her hating the people she lived with. Even if she were neurotic I could understand some of the reasons why.

A name and an address: Lucia Melho. Garvin Street.

I made a U-turn and headed down to M Street and onto Pennsylvania. Beyond the Capitol I cut through Seward Square, turning off finally just short of the Marine Barracks.

It was an old part of town, fashionable in the time of Jefferson Davis, now largely run-down, seedy and scraggly. Hardly a street light to a block. Holes in the street, junk piled at the curb. A sag-front grocery advertised its specials in white water paint across the grimy window. A small corner bar and poolroom. Dark faces. Husky voices drifted out into the night. Lucia Melho. Pensioned by Baron Alejandro Esquivel, con man and thief. What did she know of the past? What did she have that could help Megan?

From the street only an occasional house number. I would have to look on foot. I parked near a street light and locked the car.

The houses were paintless clapboard or false-front brick, crouched like old blind dogs. Borders of knee-high hedges lifted their branches in a prayer for rain they could no longer use. In the distance a locomotive whistle bludgeoned the night like a heavy saber.

The number was tacked to the front porch. A screened porch with an iron swing, oilcloth covering thin padding. Something brushed my leg and I almost yelped, but it was only a cat. It meowed plaintively, hungrily and scratched the screen.

I rang the bell and heard the buzzer sound off in the back of the house. Not much of a place for a pensioner of the Baron Esquivel. A shabby finale after Old World luxury.

I pushed the button again and realized that the house was entirely dark. My eyes were adjusting to the darkness. I opened the screen door enough to let the cat slither through. It padded over the porch boards and disappeared through the front door. It seemed to know the way. A hungry cat and the hour long past dinner.

Lighting a cigarette, I held the flame near the house number. It was the number Megan had written. Check.

The screen door had been unlatched, the front door was partly open. Lucia wouldn't have gone to bed or left the house unlocked. She could have dozed after dinner. I pushed the button again, heard it chatter hollowly. Still nothing. I cupped my hands and put them against the screen. "Hello. Anyone home?"

Silence.

A soft padding on the porch. The cat again, back arched furrily. It looked up at me and meowed. Still hungry. No food in her plate.

Turning, I looked around. The street was empty. On either side the houses were dark. Asleep and saving electricity or vacant.

The cat meowed again. I opened the screen door to let it out but it turned and ran back into the house. In that moment I made up my mind. I opened the door the rest of the way, hinges screeching, and stepped inside.

In my pocket was a pencil flash. Before I crossed the threshold I turned it on.

A bare dusty floor, cracks in the floor big enough for a fat mouse. A cockroach waddled away from the bright beam. There was a table and a TV, fairly new; a daybed and a doorway leading off to the kitchen. I flashed the light around for a wall switch and as I found it I stopped. Breath gurgled in my throat.

A woman was sitting in a rocker. A woman in a gray cotton dress, black stockings and black buttoned shoes. A woman nearer seventy than sixty. An old woman with gray hair and dusky skin, hands in her lap. The cat jumped into her lap, nosed the fingers and jumped down again. Along the back of my head the hair rose like quills.

The little beam showed the old lady's throat. All of it. The chin pointed upward and the head lay back over the top of the rocker. It was a position no one could hold in life, but now she was beyond all pain, beyond all discomfort. From where I stood the eyes were hidden. I didn't want to see them. I knew what would be in them: deep, vacant staring horror. I had seen the look too often. The neck would be broken, snapped like a carrot.

Tiptoeing forward I tried to lift one arm but it was as stiff as an angle iron.

The cat yowled again and my scalp lifted.

I took away my hand and walked past the rocker and its burden. There was a kitchen with dishes in the sink. A half-filled milk bottle stood on the drain-board. Under the kerosene stove was a chipped china saucer. I filled it with milk and scratched for the kitten. It came running, crouched beside the saucer and began emptying it. I got out my handkerchief, polished my prints from the milk bottle and replaced it.

The bedroom held a single bed. The mattress had been slashed and gutted. Bureau drawers had been overturned, dumped on the mattress. In the corner an old-fashioned round-topped trunk had been violated. Its ancient lock had been sprung open, the contents torn out.

I went back into the front room and played the light around looking for a telephone that wasn't there. The room was hot and fetid. I ran my finger under my collar and wiped the sweat on my sleeve. Then I squeezed through the front door, crossed the sagging porch and pushed aside the screen door. Before I went down the walk I paused in the shadows to scan the street. Nothing but indistinguishable voices from the poolroom on the corner.

I thought I saw a flash of motion on the other side of the street, as though someone had moved behind a tree. But as I watched the street was as immobile as ever. Optical tricks. Too long in darkness. I wiped sweat from my forehead and went out to the old slab sidewalk. From there I walked slowly to the Olds, unlocked it and got in. Before I started the engine I swallowed two ounces from the glove compartment and then I pulled away from the curb, past the house where in life old Lucia Melho had lived.

I drove two blocks before switching on my headlights. Turning south I stopped in front of a package store near the Naval Gun Factory. A dime in the phone booth got me Police Headquarters. The desk sergeant switched me to Kellaway's office and after a pause I heard his frayed voice. "Kellaway, Homicide. What'll it be?"

"A corpse on Garvin street."

"Yeah? That you, Steve?"

"No kidding."

"All right. Get the hell down here right now. And no drinking on the way."

CHAPTER SIX

"So you just tiptoed in for the hell of it, violating every known law and ordinance on the way, and a kitty-cat led you to the corpse." His voice was as sour as a green quince. Picking up a cardboard coffee container, he drained cold dregs and tossed it at a corner basket. The shot missed. He glared at the rolling container and made a sucking sound with his teeth.

I said, "That's how it was."

"Yeah? Just what the hell were you doing down in that part of town that time of night, Steve? Don't say coincidence or I'm liable to break your neck with these two hands."

"You cops are always complaining the town's badly patrolled. I've always agreed with you. Let's say I was putting in a volunteer hour. Checking Garvin Street."

Kellaway flicked up his hat ten degrees and leaned forward. His strong fingers laced together like knotted rope. "See my hands?" he asked in a guttural voice. "I'm keeping them like this so they won't do you any harm. Don't push me. I've had a bitch of a day with the D.A. and right now I could bite through a baseball bat like it was spaghetti."

"Hell, I thought you ate them for breakfast. With catchers' mitts for dessert."

He glared at me with red-rimmed eyes. "For two days I've had no sleep worth the name. Sometimes I get a bang out of light chatter but this is the wrong time and the wrong place."

"Like the Korean War."

"Yeah. Now when I was only a lieutenant I didn't mind playing fast and loose with you and maybe cutting corners now and then but, goddammit, I'm a captain now and if they catch me fooling around with guys suppressing evidence they'll break my back and bury the pieces."

"Oh, balls," I said, got out my pipe, filled it and lighted it. "A client asked me to take a message out to her. I tried but the old lady was beyond listening."

"What was the message?"

"She was to give me anything she had for my client."

"I see," he said in an ominous voice. His fingers unwound and became two clenched fists. One of them slammed the desk like a mallet. "Goddammit, I want that client's name! I want everything you know and I want it fast!"

I stood up and took the pipe out of my mouth. "Simmer down. You'll get all I have when there's enough to be of use to you. Right now there's nothing. Take it or leave it." Turning, I began to walk toward the door.

"Come back here!" he shouted.

I halted. "On what terms?"

"Yours," he said grudgingly. "What the hell else?"

I shot him a winning smile and pulled the car pint from my side pocket. "You're on edge," I said as I sat down again. "Nerves. I don't feel too calm myself. Let's sort of finish this baby off and see how we feel then."

"Lock the door," Kellaway growled.

When I came back he was dividing the end of the pint between two fogged drinking glasses.

He handed me one and said, "Nuts to the District Commissioners."

"Mothballs in their gas tanks."

We drank Kellaway pushed his hat back a little further and looked at the glass with a pleased expression. "This certainly came from the right keg. Now, what were we talking about?"

"We were saying how glad I'll be to give you anything I have—when I have anything useful."

"Yeah, that," he said. "Well, the M.E. says a broken neck, like you figured. No finger marks on the throat, though. He figures the guy was behind her and did it with the crook of his arm under the chin."

"Why a guy?"

"It takes some strength to do that," he said patiently and wet his throat again. "Not many women would have that kind of strength."

"Ever see a female weight-lifter or a lady wrestler?"

"Sure. But how many of them you got distributed through the population?"

"Too many for me."

"I got to agree with you there." He lifted the glass again and sipped slowly.

I said, "Any new tush hogs in town?"

"Trains come and go every day. The highways and airports are wide open. Who you got in mind?"

I described my office visitor and Kellaway shook his head. Then he said, "That tie in to the latest corpse?"

"Maybe."

"You'll let me know, won't you?" he simpered. "Any small clue you can spare."

"Count on me."

He glared at me again, lifted his glass and drained it. "Man," he said, "I had a thirst like a cotton-picker." Setting down the glass, he shuffled through some official forms and held one up. In a thoughtful voice he said, "You know your way in and around Georgetown, Steve. Maybe you could give me a lead on this."

"Shoot."

"Fellow called in today, said his life was in danger and asked for police protection. He was sure enough scared."

"What did you do?"

"Oh, we sent a plainie around to talk to him but he wasn't talking. We got a detail near the house now but we can't tie up policemen forever because some guy's got a guilty conscience. Or even just the shakes. I thought you might have heard of him. He lives up on R Street. Bought the old Falconer morgue not too far back."

"I may have," I said carefully. "If it's a man who owns a string of golden pearls."

Kellaway squinted at me across the top of the report form. "Who's kiddin' who? I've heard of everything *but* golden pearls."

"Well," I said, "there was some talk around the papers about them. Didn't he mention them?"

"Nothing here," Kellaway said. "Foreign fellow. A Baron. Name of Esquivel."

"He owns a Delahaye," I said. "I've seen it in the drive."

"Nothing else?"

"Nothing that might help you."

"I'll put it another way. Do you know anything about him that might conceivably be of interest to me?"

I picked up my glass and finished the last few drops. Twirling it in my fingers, I said, "That's asking for a subjective judgment. Any man owning an expensive string of pearls or anything else of high value and extreme salability might have cause for worry."

"He didn't ask to have any pearls protected. He asked protection for his life."

"Maybe he just got confused," I said. "You know how flustered foreigners get when they see a dial phone."

"I do?"

"Everyone does." I got up, set down the glass and said, "Unless you're detaining me for unspecified charges, I'm on my way."

"To where?"

"Bed. Why?"

He sat back in his swivel chair, selected a toothpick and stuck it between his teeth. "I thought you might have some idea about dropping back to Garvin Street. Just to see if you could locate what the thief might have missed."

I shook my head. "The thief had a world of time. Anyone smart enough to snap a neck and ransack a house without leaving a single print is smart enough to find any hiding place the old lady might have thought of."

"What would she have been hiding, Steve?"

"Who knows?"

"Try a little harder," he said cynically. "You can do better than that. I know."

"Well, she could have stuck away her Eastern Star credentials or a stack of Confederate money or a poke full of polar-bear teeth."

"Sweet dreams, baby," he said heavily. "Don't choke on a polar-bear tooth."

When I got out to my car it was wet with condensation. I used my handkerchief to clear the windshield and tossed the soggy square behind the seat. The engine was slow to start and when it finally caught I was thinking about why the Baron had asked for police protection and hardly noticed the engine running. I pulled away from the curb, drove two blocks to Yateman's package store and ducked in for a pint of the old and amber. When it was tucked away intact in the glove compartment, I headed north, out Massachusetts Avenue. Time: twelve after eleven. Switching on the radio I caught the quarter hour sportscast. Slim Spokane had won on a tko in the sixth round. The news made me feel a little better. If I had gone I would have put ten on the other boy. That put me ten ahead for the night. But that was all.

. On the debit side was Megan Dos Santos, her strange life and hatreds; the message I was to have delivered to Lucia Melho, and finally the corpse itself. It was no time of night to call Megan even if it had been the thing to do. She could read it in the morning papers, or if she missed she could learn it from me tomorrow night. Hell, it was nearly tomorrow already. The murder of old Lucia Melho was more than just coincidence. Death played strange games but she was killed by no chance looter. She was killed because of things she knew; because of what she was to have given me. Whatever it was only two people knew now: Megan and the murderer.

By lying to Kellaway I had kept Megan out of it for the time being. There would be ways to trace Lucia Melho back to the Baron's household but probably none to connect the old servant directly to Megan. Unless Megan decided to tell the police. And that seemed unlikely. The story she told me could have been dreamed up by a hysterical girl, a sympathy-seeker with a neurotic self-dramatizing bent. It had the trappings of drama and fiction: sudden death, poverty, riches, fraud and deceit and menace. Foreign places with strange-sounding names. Beauty and death and pearls. Golden pearls. Cheated men with blood grudges against their defrauder. Movies had been made on less. And yet, as I thought of the girl, remembering her face and her eyes and her voice, there was nothing of the compulsive liar about her.

I liked the thought of the Baron calling for police protection. The same police could protect Megan if anything or anyone threatened her. And it wasn't only the chauffeur that worried me.

The broad avenue was as shiny as wet licorice. The Embassy cocktail parties were over and where the dinner parties were well along there were clumps of limousines with chauffeurs slumped behind the wheel or leaning on the fender, smoking and staring up at the sky. As I drove past the Cathedral the moon broke from behind the clouds and silhouetted the spires and the gray Gothic bulk. I yawned, blinked and sat forward on the seat to stay awake. I was dead tired but it was more mental than physical. The day had been a long one and varied. Not to mention confusing. It would stand for a long time as unique. I wondered if Artie's boys had discovered anything interesting about the Baron's chauffeur. And I wondered if there was even anything interesting to learn. He could be just a uniformed pug doubling as a driver.

Nothing more. Or he could be a good deal more. I was too tired to speculate. If there was anything to be known Artie would tell me. Tomorrow.

I drove the Olds down the garage ramp below the apartment building and let the attendant park it for me.

The clerk was nodding behind the desk so I reached over and pulled my key from the box. A fine attentive lad with a big future as a floorwalker. I wondered how long he'd waited for the Syrian delegation and their goats.

Riding up in the elevator I rested my weight on the hand rail and when it stopped at my floor I stumbled out into the dimly-lighted hall. I was twirling the key in my hand and thinking of nothing except how much I wanted to hit the sack, when I stopped at my door and saw a figure on the floor, leaning back into the offset, hands around her knees. At first I thought it was Megan, but then I saw shimmering platinumed hair. She yawned, covering her mouth, and extended one hand. I pulled her upright and she leaned against me the way she had earlier in the day. "Where have you been?" she asked in a piqued voice.

"Oh, out and around. Anything I can do for you?"

"You can make me a drink."

I put the key in the lock, turned it and murmured, "What would Alejandro think?"

"You know the answer to that: does anyone really care?"

I pushed the door inward and she glided past me and into the darkness. I followed, shut the door with my heel and reached for the light switch. Instead, her arms were around me and her lips were on mine, hot and dry and insistent. Her tongue was a river of fire. We kissed long enough to exhaust a limited subject and then I pulled her hands apart and switched on the light.

She was wearing a wrap-around polo coat, a formfitting black silk dress and a necklace of round beads colored dusty gold. With a movement of her shoulders she slid out of the polo coat and let it drop to the floor. She put her hands on her hips, spread her legs apart and said, "Aren't you glad I'm here?"

I walked across to the bar, switched on the light and pulled out the makings. "Ice?" I asked.

She shook her head, then fingered the feathery hair back into place.

I said, "I thought a cooler might be indicated. The temperature seemed to be rising."

She laughed. "It could have kept on rising."

"We weren't far from the boiling point. Me, I'll have a little ice." I went into the kitchen, broke cubes from a tray and came back. When the drinks were ready I handed the unadulterated one to her and touched the glass with mine. *"A la vôtre,"* I said, "and all that sort of rot."

She drank briefly, laughed and said, "You respect nothing, do you?"

"Very little."

"That might be why I like you."

"You like me, Anita?"

A little frown appeared. "Do you think I would let you kiss me if I did not like you—very much?"

"Back to the beginning," I said. "Who's been kissing whom? If memory serves me, you've been doing the kissing and I've been permitting it. Not that it hasn't been barrels of fun."

That worried her even more. She gave me an uncertain glance. Gliding toward me she linked her arm with mine and drew me toward the sofa. She fell into it as though it were an old and tested friend. Looking up, she said, "You are probably the most impolite man I have ever known."

"Sorry," I said, sitting beside her. "I'll have to work on my manners. Any books you could recommend?"

She made a little face, sipped her drink and changed the subject. "Are you not pleased to find me here?"

"You've asked me that. Well, I'm bowled over. It isn't every night I stagger home and find heaven curled up on my threshold."

She gave a light liquid laugh. "That's much better." Her glass clinked against mine. "To us."

"I'd like to drink to that," I said, "if only I knew what it meant. Not too many hours ago a man came to my office. He was big enough for a circus wrestler and he wore a cream-colored raincoat and a college-boy hat. Only he wasn't clowning, Anita. He had a gun."

"A gun?" She sat forward, her face tight.

"Very much of a gun."

"Did he rob you?"

"He gave me some advice. Since it affects us I might as well tell you what he said."

"Please do." Her hand was tight around the glass. Her knuckles looked like polished ivory.

"Well," I said, and sipped my drink, "he told me to stay away from your house. A simple message. He didn't really need to repeat it, but he did. The way he emphasized it—and the fact that he brought a gun to help make his point—convinced me he was sincere."

"Who was the man?" she breathed.

"I wish I knew. Then, again, I might be better off not knowing. The thought occurred to me that Alejandro could have hired him to keep undesirable people from molesting you."

She shook her head slowly. "You think you are undesirable?"

"I've been told differently on occasion."

"And this man has frightened you?"

"He threw a small shiver into me. Besides, I had no reason to return to your home. Not even to examine your husband's fine collection of antique pistols—I assumed his invitation was only a formality."

"Of course."

I leaned back against the cushion and looked down at my glass. "So you see, if I haven't violated the letter of the man's advice, your being here certainly goes against the spirit of it."

"This worries you?" she asked with a shade of scorn.

"When I think about it, it does." I lifted my glass, touched hers and said, "Let's not think about it."

That brought a sunny smile. She lifted her knees and brought her legs onto the cushions. Somehow her shoes slipped onto the rug. Her free hand went behind her neck and did something to the necklace clasp. The strand came free and she laid it across one thigh. "The golden pearls," she said quietly. "I thought you might like to see them."

I pinched the clasp between my thumb and forefinger and lifted the strand nearer the light. Then I put the smallest pearl between my teeth and bit lightly. Her eyebrows lifted in surprise. The surface of the pearl was gritty. That made it a real pearl. An artificial one would have been hard and smooth. Leaning across, I laid the strand on the end table. Under the light the pearls looked like dusty gold as old as time itself.

I said, "It was thoughtful to bring them."

"You like them?"

"Very much."

She smiled. "I was sure you would. They are mine, you know. My husband gave them to me."

"He looks like a man who could buy a lot of things," I said. "Even love. Or what passes for it."

Her hand lashed out and struck the side of my face. Her eyes were slits. The hand dropped away. "I ... I'm sorry. I did not mean to hurt you. Dut what you said—"

"What I said I meant. A small thimble would hold all the love you feel for old spade-beard. And don't try to tell me differently."

Her face had gone white. Her lips trembled and she swallowed more of her drink. But when she lowered the glass she was under control again. “I agree,” she said evenly. “Why should I lie? I would prefer you knew the truth.”

I cupped my left hand around the back of her head. Her eyes fluttered and her lips parted.

I said, “I have few scruples but breaking up happy marriages is one of them.”

“There is no danger of that,” she whispered thickly. “In our marriage there is no happiness.” Then her lips covered mine and her mouth opened hotly. As I leaned forward to turn out the light, she fell back against the cushion. In the moving darkness I could hear the rustle of silk, the soft sliding of a zipper, and then her naked arms were winding around my neck. Her nipples were as hard as rubies.

CHAPTER SEVEN

I woke and the room was cold. The bedclothes were pulled aside. I was alone. I rattled out of bed like an anchor chain and closed the window. The table clock said ten after two. I went into the empty living room and bolted the front door. The pearls were gone, too. *Adios, Anita.* Does the Baron know or doesn't he care? Not that I'd ever get the truth from you, my platinum nymph.

I had wanted to talk about her life in Europe, check, if possible, Megan's story. But it had not been a night for sustained conversation. Still, there might be others. Holding the thought, I got back into bed and pulled up the covers. After a while the bed got warm again and I fell asleep.

When I reached the office it was nine-thirty and disapproval was engraved deep in Mrs. Bross's face. I ignored it, slid behind my desk and burrowed into a stack of work. When I found myself making errors I got up, went down to the street and bought a morning paper. In the elevator I thumbed through the pages and found a short paragraph on page eighteen. It told of Lucia Melho's murder, starkly with no details. Nothing of her origins. There was still some police footwork before any of that emerged. Back at my desk I put aside the paper, hoping Megan would read the notice. It would save me breaking the cold news when I saw her tonight.

I was holding out on Kellaway only until I knew how much helping him would hurt Megan. I didn't mind Homicide questioning Megan so long as it was done away from Police Headquarters and grinning reporters. The law could get satisfaction without putting her through the wringer. Or so I told myself.

The door opened and Mrs. Bross peeked in. "Mr. Von Amond to see you."

I nodded and she stood aside. Artie brushed past her and the door closed. Tossing his hat at a chair, he sat down and said, "What kind of a chase have I been on, Steve?"

"The usual."

"See the morning paper?"

I pointed at the one on my desk.

"Just once I'd like to have you break clean with me. According to Immigration the Baron entered the States seven months ago with his wife, Anita, and her half-sister, Megan Dos Santos. And a maidservant named Melho. Lucia Melho." He put his elbows on the desk and leaned forward. "Whaddaya know—this morning Lucia Melho turns up dead. Neck cracked by a prowler—or so the papers say." His face went sour. "As if you didn't know."

"Think I knew she was going to be murdered?"

"There's a hell of a lot of coincidence somewhere," he said bitterly. "You told Kellaway?"

"I had to. I found the body."

His jaw dropped, he pushed away from the desk and stared at me. He wet his lips. "Last night?"

I nodded.

He fumbled for a cigarette, lighted it and blew smoke across my desk. "Who did it?"

"Nobody knows. Except the murderer."

"What in hell's it all about, Steve?"

I took a pipe from the rack, filled and lighted it. When it was going well I leaned back in my chair and told him. It took a little telling, and more than a little while. When I had finished I shook ashes from my pipe and waited for him to say something. What he said was, "You get tied up in the goddamndest things."

"And some people are accident-prone. A smart astrologer would have an explanation."

"None that would satisfy me." He pulled a report sheet from his pocket and laid it on my desk. "There's the known statistics on the Esquivel family, all three." He took out another report and cleared his throat. "The boys tailed your chauffeur buddy last night. As soon as it got dark he drove the Delahaye across town and picked up a guy down in Chinatown. Fellow over six feet tall with a light-colored fly-front raincoat and a crushed rain hat. One of the lads said he looked like an out-of-town hood named Ducky Macaluso, but the light was bad for a certain make."

"The description fits a pistolero who dropped by here last evening, braced me and told me to stay the hell away from the R Street house. For the sake of argument let's say he was Big Al's passenger."

"You neglected to mention that little bit."

"It was after hours. By then you had your socks off, watching TV."

"I should be so lucky." He looked down at the report again. "They rode around for a while, parked the buggy in a lot near the Hotel Bedford and went up to Room seven-nineteen. Ten minutes later Macaluso—if that's who he was—comes down. Welinsky don't come down for another half hour. When he does, he heads for an ale house and begins pounding them down for another hour. After that he staggers out of the grill and drives the big buggy back to Georgetown."

"Home for the night?"

"Not by a damn sight. He parks up on P Street and walks over to Avon Place. Some reconditioned houses there they made over into small apartments. This one had four, two on each floor. The lads couldn't make out which one he went into. Or why."

"How long was he there?"

"Maybe all night. The boys went home at twelve."

I sat forward. "Why?"

"Why? Because that's when tail jobs end. Unless you want two teams and after midnight it's double money."

"We weren't talking money, we were talking coverage."

"You want two teams on him?"

"Not anymore."

His face screwed up. "If you had any ideas Welinsky broke the old girl's neck this sort of cleans him, no?"

"Your boys only picked him up at nightfall. By then Lucia could have been dead."

"What's the M.E. say?"

"He hasn't confided in me. But it was a cold, cold corpse with a flowering case of rigor. When I found her she'd been dead no little while."

He looked uncomfortable. "If you'd told me what to—"

"Hell, I didn't know myself. Who was in seven-nine-teen at the Bedford?"

He brightened. "A man named Garaldo. Mario Garaldo. According to the house man he'd be about five nine or ten and heavy-built. A trim dresser, buffed nails, slick pepper-and-salt hair and a gold cap on one front tooth. Where he's from and what he does didn't come out. You got ideas?"

"Yesterday afternoon the Baron called in for police protection. Said his life was in danger."

"For why?"

"He didn't specify."

"Account of the pearls?"

I shrugged. "The Baron doesn't confide in me either. According to Kellaway there's a detail covering the house now."

"Thanks," Artie said dryly. "I guess you don't care if my boys get run in for loitering."

"I hadn't given it much thought."

"It's getting to be a pretty crowded area up there. Cops watching who goes in and my boys watching who comes out. How long's the detail going to hang around?"

"Couple of days. Just long enough to give satisfaction."

Artie stood up, placed his palms on the desk and said, "This isn't the same case it started out to be. There's murder in it now, and a gun-packer we'll call Ducky Macaluso. What's in it for you?"

"A few bruises. Maybe worse."

His nails drummed against the desk. "How many lives you got to play with? Think you're King of the Cats?"

"I don't think about it."

"Well," Artie said, "it's Kellaway's case now. Let him handle it."

"This is a dull racket I'm in. Money and taxes. There must be more than that in life."

"You should live so long," Artie said. "I'll call in from time to time—providing, of course, I got any boys left outside the jail house."

He picked up his hat, twirled it a couple of times and sidled out of the office. The door closed. I got up, walked around the desk and stared down across the street at the gray statue of Alexander Hamilton. Pigeons were pecking restlessly around the stone pediment. Beyond it the White House gates were open to shuffling lines of tourists. For no observable reason the pigeons abandoned Hamilton and spiraled upward and away in the direction of the river. Apparently aimless flight, but something had triggered it; sixth sense, instinct, radar, call it by any name. The quest for food, the approach of a storm, danger.

Picking up the directory I found a number and dialed the Hotel Bedford and asked for room seven-nineteen. After a while a heavy, accented voice said "Yes?"

"Room service," I said in a nasal voice. "Order, please."

"I did not call."

"Sorry, sir." I hung up. Mario Garaldo was home.

I wondered what his plans for the day might be. Whether they included Al Welinsky or the man called Macaluso, or both. Or neither.

The work on my desk looked as inviting as last week's lentil soup. I went out of the office, got the Olds out of the garage and drove over 14th Street. Parking a block away from the Bedford I pushed through the doors into the lobby.

It was a hotel not old but no longer new, built when beige brick was all the rage. Sofas and chair backs stained with hair oil, a couple of tired window boxes and a seedy-looking pansy behind the desk. I stuck a nickel in the self-service newspaper rack and pulled out a morning paper. Then I strolled over to one of the chairs and sat down. The bell captain was an inch over five feet tall, with a face like a John Bull beer mug and eyes as shiny as the casques of scarab beetles. He was perched on a bench, drumming his nails on his knees and waiting for the ceiling to cave in. After a while his eyes roved around and settled on me. I crooked a finger. He glanced at the desk clerk, got up slowly and idled over. The clerk kept on sorting room keys.

I said, "How's business?"

"Like the market. Got its ups and downs."

"I'd like a little assistance."

"Dame?" I thought he was going to dribble on me.

"Never before noon. Fellow in seven-nineteen, foreigner. Make him?"

His face screwed up, he squinted at the ceiling, his face relaxed and he looked down at me. "What's the gaff? Copper?"

I pulled a fiver from my pocket and palmed it to him. It disappeared like a leaf in a high gale. A smile grew on his midget face. "That's an answer gets things done."

"Bank protective agency," I said. "He's cashing a lot of checks. Someone thought it might be a buildup. Any other ideas?"

He shook his head slowly. "Looks legit from what I see. Could be otherwise but no reason to think so. That's not much for a fin."

"The rest's easy. He ought to be coming down for lunch pretty soon. You can finger him for me."

"I'm off at two."

"That'll be long enough."

"Okay. The name's Chester. I been here six years. Any little jobs you need done keep me in mind. I dig this place better than the termites."

He strolled back to the bench and sat down. His eyes went as blank as etched glass. I started on the editorial page and had the first editorial finished when an elderly couple dragged in and claimed their key at the desk. Then two salesmen conning each other over the size of their last sale. One editorial later, a blonde who could have been a hooker but whose mouth was bitter enough for marriage. Next a suffering father with two small sons in Indian suits. The lads whooped and wailed until the father backhanded one of them into silence. The clerk glared at them as they trooped toward the elevator and I remembered Bill Field's appraisal: for a man who hates animals and small children there's always hope.

Then ten minutes of somber silence. Finally the elevator door opened and three people came out: the elderly couple and a short solidly-built man in a dark pin-striped suit, dove-gray hat, and black, pointed oxfords. He walked past the desk without dropping off his key and Chester stood up. He coughed loudly and made a quick gesture with his hand. I nodded, folded my paper and strolled out of the door. While the doorman was whistling down a cab I jogged down the block and got into the Olds. A cab stopped at the hotel entrance, the man got in and the cab drove away. Pulling out from the curb, I followed.

The cab went north as far as R Street, then west and around Sheridan Circle, over the bridge and up 28th to R again. A block from the old Falconer house the cab slowed and I saw the passenger move over toward the window. An all-black Chevrolet was parked near the iron gate. It could have been an ordinary civilian car but for the Whip aerial mounted on the rear fender. The car and its occupants were as inconspicuous as rouge on a parson's collar. The cops might not trap many people but they could certainly frighten them away.

The cab picked up speed, went as far as Wisconsin and turned south. At M Street it turned again, heading back for downtown. I followed as far as Connecticut and caught a stop light. When the light changed the cab was lost from sight. I swore, turned up Connecticut and merged with the creeping traffic.

For a fin I had learned what Mario Garaldo looked like. Even more important, that he was interested in Baron Esquivel's digs. It seemed like a lot for the price. I wondered who Garaldo was, why he had come to Washington and why he had received two gutter rats like Al Welinsky and Ducky Macaluso in his rooms last evening. I turned the car into a lot on De Sales Street and crossed to the Mayflower. From a lobby booth I called Kellaway.

"Well, well," he said icily, "is this the honorable recording secretary of the Baker Street Irregulars, District Branch? Or possibly Mycroft Holmes, himself, to volunteer a few inscrutable clues?"

"Don't get all sententious," I told him. "I haven't had the courage to join anything since they booted me out of DeMolay for throwing spitballs. Now if we can get back to matters at hand, you might be interested in learning that there's a husky torpedo in town who's been made as Ducky Macaluso. That mean anything to you?"

"Hoods come and go. What's Macaluso in your young life?"

"I thought he might be one of Maury Renzo's boys."

"That's no distinction. If he's Ducky he broke in with Maury, worked as an arm around Baltimore a while and drifted out of the area."

"You might check the fliers. Just to see if anyone wants him anywhere."

"That," Kellaway said, "is police work." His tone became suspicious. "You telling me all you know?"

"That would take hours. Chew on what you've got. We'll talk later."

"We'd better," he said and rang off.

I stepped out of the booth, walked across the lobby and entered the Snake Pit. While I was stirring my scotch I counted one Vice Admiral, two Air Force Generals, an unsuccessful presidential candidate, four national columnists and a scattering of ambassadors and industrialists. At one table a dozen elderly hens clucked over the high alcoholic content in their claret punch. The ladies wore corsages and plastic name cards. They were from Lancaster, Pennsylvania, and they were living dangerously.

After a while the waiter brought me a seafood casserole and a salad. When everything was neatly tucked away I left, ransomed the Olds from the lot and drove back to my office.

Opening the outer door, I saw a man sitting in the reception room, leafing through a magazine. He put it aside and looked up at me.

He was a man with silver-gray hair, nails as shiny as new dimes, and a Continental goatee. Baron Alejandro Esquivel.

CHAPTER EIGHT

I said, "Come in, Baron."

He got up and strode into my office. I gave Mrs. Bross the do-not-disturb wink and closed the door. The Baron turned and his eyes followed me as I went behind my desk and sat down. He cleared his throat. A little nervously for a Baron.

I wondered if he knew where Anita had frolicked last night or if he was aware that Megan had met me clandestinely. If so, the subject was his to open. I filled my pipe, lighted it and waited.

He was sitting in a chair, leaning forward slightly. I blew smoke at the window and let my eyebrows go up slowly.

The Baron cleared his throat again. I felt like offering him menthol lozenges. Possibly it was only nervousness. A man who had asked the police to protect his life might have reason to be nervous.

His right thumb and index finger began to rotate together. His eyes followed my line of sight until he noticed what his fingers were doing. He started, smiled weakly and said, "Mr. Bentley, I have come to you for some advice."

"What sort of advice, Baron? Financial?"

He leaned farther forward. I was going to get the really confidential treatment. At least he wasn't cuffing me with a glove and demanding satisfaction at dawn.

"In a sense financial, since it concerns my possessions."

"The District *ad valorem* tax?"

He shook his head slowly. "I wish it were that simple. No, Mr. Bentley, it has to do with my pearls."

"The golden pearls?"

He nodded with a slight pleased smile.

I said, "There shouldn't be any tax problem with them, Baron. I understand they were brought in under bond, and—"

One hand lifted. "Please. I had better tell you exactly what is troubling me."

I sat back, clamped down on my pipe stem and got ready to listen. Glancing over his shoulder at the closed door, he turned back to me. "My pearls are worth some appraisers say as much as one hundred thousand dollars. They are insured for less but that does not affect their true value—and in any case I am not interested in their sale. I am interested in keeping them."

"What's there to—?"

The hand lifted again. "It may sound incredible to you, sir, but I have reason to fear that they will be stolen from me."

I remembered Kellaway's guard detail, and was about to guffaw when his jaw stuck out challengingly and he said tightly, "Not by some common thief, but from within my own household."

I blinked. His lips curled into a condescending sneer and he said, "Yes. Incredible as it may sound."

I took my pipe from between my teeth and lowered it. "Perhaps I don't understand exactly why you came to me, Baron. I'm a CPA and a tax adviser. I have nothing to do with stolen jewels, much less the prevention of theft. Your problem is one for the police—or for a private detective."

He cleared his throat again. This time he gave me a winning smile. "I came to see you, Mr. Bentley, because you appear to me to be a man of character. I have not lived in this country long enough to have a wide acquaintanceship among persons of character and confidence."

"I appreciate the compliment. Would you mind telling me why you feel I have the sort of character you mention?"

His hands spread, palms out. "Simplicity itself. What you did for Megan was the act of a man of character. Including your misguided attempt to protect her from Wells."

My spine stiffened.

He said, "In brief, I thought you might be able to recommend to me someone in whom I might repose confidence; someone to whom I could confide my problem and who at the same time would be competent to take the necessary steps to protect me."

"Why not let the insurers know, Baron? They'd be more than interested in protecting the pearls against theft."

A slight sigh escaped him. "If you have tried in recent years to insure expensive jewelry against theft or loss you will know that it is a difficult matter to accomplish. The rates are fabulously high and the insurance companies are extraordinarily selective. I should prefer not to prejudice my insurance in any way and informing the insurers could, unfortunately, serve that purpose. Now, do you know someone you might recommend?"

"The District Detective Agency," I said. "It's run by a Mr. Arthur Von Amond. I think he can meet your specifications in full."

His face relaxed and he stood up. "I am infinitely obliged to you, sir. If there is a charge for this consultation, I would be delighted to pay."

"No charge."

He bowed slightly. "I am in your debt."

"On the contrary," I said, thinking of Anita.

He looked at me oddly. One finger tapped the rim of his hat and he said, "If you would call me when you have some free time I would be glad to show you my collection of pistols. Some of them would be of particular interest to someone who knows firearms."

"At the first opportunity." I stood up.

"Good day, Mr. Bentley," he said, turned and went out of the office. When the door snapped shut I went into the reception room and stared at the closed door. Mrs. Bross said, "A very distinguished-looking gentleman. Is he your client now?"

"In a way," I said. "But very indirectly."

"I'm afraid I don't understand, Mr. Bentley."

"He's an alien resident, Mrs. Bross, so his tax problems are few and far between. His big problems are of a different type." I looked down at her. "Supposing you had a set of sparklers and you had reason to believe that they might be stolen—what would you do?"

"Put them in my safe deposit box."

"Exactly," I said, and went back into my office.

Picking up my pipe, I knocked off the dead ashes, lighted it and sat down.

At first the stage had been relatively empty, the characters definable. Now the scene was as crowded as a Robbins sidewalk ballet. Plus unseen others working backstage. I was willing to accept the Baron's picture of me as a man of character—within limits and excluding cuckoldry—but as an explanation for his visit it was too facile. I picked up the phone, got Artie and told him to expect a visit from the Baron.

"What's his problem?"

"I don't think he's likely to be entirely frank. But what he'll ask you to do is guard those golden pearls of his."

"That oughta be a cupcake—with Kellaway's men staked out all over the scenery."

"He's not worried about any strolling Jimmy Valentine, Artie. He gave me to believe the threat came from inside the house. Anyway, let me know what he says."

"Sure thing."

"This fellow Garaldo—the guy in seven-nineteen at the Bedford—took a slow cruise past the Baron's house earlier today. So there's that for the pot as well."

Artie whistled. "Know anything about Garaldo?"

"No. But the Baron might."

"He might at that. I might even ask him."

"Use your own judgment."

"That I'll do."

He hung up and I replaced the receiver.

If there was one thing about the Baron that stood out, it was his indirectness. He was devious. He was smooth as polished ebony and twice as opaque. If what he had told me was in any part the truth, it raised some interesting speculations. What had made him think the pearls were in danger of being stolen? By whom? Molly? Wells-Welinsky? Anita? Or Megan? Or was the inside slant a lead away from Mario Garaldo?

I had meant to ask him where he kept the jewels but the moment had passed without the question being asked. Houses of that generation were built with safes of all sizes and shapes and I had seen some with vaults big enough for a wine-cellar.

There was another way to look at the Baron's visit: no threat to the pearls existed. None except from him. If he were planning to have the pearls disappear and collect on their insurance, what better way to allay suspicion than to hire professional protection in advance? It had been done before. Insurance investigators' files were filled with that kind of attempted fraud. Pulling it off took a special sort of skill plus blood as cold as Arctic seas. I had the feeling that the Baron might possess both.

Knocking the dottle from my pipe, I put it back on the rack and stared at the wall. If the Baron knew Lucia Melho was dead he had given me no indication. But then he would have no reason to know that I was involved. I wished that Megan had told me more about what she had hoped to get from Lucia Melho, and against what or whom she was trying to protect herself. I had been only a messenger boy. D'Artagnan trying manfully to regain the queen's diamonds, unaware of Richelieu's intrigues. I shook my head. Much too dramatic. Megan could be a mentally disturbed youngster, a psycho-hysteric with a persecution complex.

Except for the fact that Lucia Melho was dead.

That was a big fact. Mountain sized. It overshadowed my doubts. Megan was no neurotic kid, but a girl with an adult size case of the shakes. In doing what she had asked, I had been justified. The point now was to find what it all meant. In the finding several points ought to be cleared up. Including who might have had reason to kill the old Portuguese pensioner.

Glancing at my phone, I found myself wishing it would ring. I wanted Megan to know that Lucia was dead and I wanted to confirm that she knew. I decided to call the house on the chance that Megan might answer. Picking up the directory, I scanned the pages for the Falconer sisters' number. Nothing there. Then Esquivel. Nothing there either. The house number was unlisted. I should have asked Megan for it last night. I should have done a lot of things last night. Other things I should have left strictly alone. Like Anita.

I thought about it for a while and then I went out to lunch.

When I got back there was a notation to call Kellaway.

His voice was burred with fatigue. "You ever work the river boats?"

"Not recently. Why?"

"Cards close to the vest. It wouldn't have hurt you to let me know the dead woman used to work for Baron Esquivel."

"Did I know that?"

"You're damned right you knew it. And that comes close to suppressing evidence."

"Not in my law-book it doesn't."

He made an unpleasant sound.

I said, "Call it a day for coincidence. Lucia Melho is dead and her former employer called you for protection. What else do you make of it?"

"I make it more than simple coincidence. Suddenly I don't like the Baron very much. I think I might just take a run over there and ask him to explain the coincidence—if such it is. We might even haul him down here and take his prints."

"You said there weren't any prints around Lucia's house."

"So I did. He doesn't need to know that though. The reason I called was to make sure I wouldn't be stumbling over you if I went to the Baron's house. He *was* the client who asked you to take the message to Lucia, wasn't he? Or had I better ask him?"

My stomach went cold.

"Well?" Kellaway said grimly. "What about it?"

"He wasn't the client."

Kellaway laughed bitterly. "Steve, right now you've got a pretty low truth rating with me. I wouldn't push it any lower."

"All right. Take his prints, bounce him off the ceiling if you want, but leave me out of it."

"Bashful?" he sneered.

"Call it that."

"Goddammit!" he roared, "you're going to break clean with me! Who got you to go to Garvin Street last night?"

I took a deep breath. "A girl," I said. "Nineteen years old. Half-sister of the Baron's wife. Lucia used to be her maid. She was afraid of something, she didn't specify what. To calm her down I agreed to see Lucia. I thought she was neurotic but the murder proves she wasn't."

"Well, well," Kellaway said silkily. "Gratitude flows from me like milk and honey in the Promised Land. How neurotic might the young lady be? Neurotic enough to break an old lady's neck?"

"That's the kind of enlightened police attitude that made me hold back her name the first time around."

"Will you give me one reasonably logical argument why?"

"I think the kid's been pushed around enough. I didn't like the thought of your boys working her over down in the big sweat box."

His voice was as rough and hard as a file. "That, again, happens to be police business. In any book of law. Now, unless you want to break off an old friendship, I'm telling you to leave murders to me. I'll handle the case myself. My own way. How I get information will be my decision, not yours. Also how I handle any suspects. Is that understood?"

"I get the drift. Now let's try it another way. Suppose you lay off the girl for, say, twenty-four hours, and let me see what I can turn up."

"The hell with you."

"What's so sensational about an old lady's neck getting cracked down on Garvin Street that you can't afford to handle the case routinely without all the hurry-up? It's only a page-eighteen crime. The Commissioner isn't sweated up about it, you aren't on a spot and there's maybe some ways I could help out. But I'll need a little time."

His voice became wary. "That implies you might just be holding out on me again."

"I might. And then again I might be in a position to do a couple of things unofficially that you'd look awfully foolish doing if they didn't happen to pan out."

"There's that," he said reluctantly. "Twenty-four hours, you said?"

"That was the figure mentioned. Dance the Baron around all night, but lay off the girl until tomorrow."

"You've got a deal," Kellaway said sorely. "I don't know why."

"Thanks for the vote of confidence. Without you around to boost my ego I'd go into a fast decline."

"Haw, haw," he jeered and hung up.

Something borrowed, something blue. Give and take. Plus a time limit slimmer than hope in Death Row. I had myself a deal.

I pulled out a handkerchief and mopped my face. Where the hell was Artie's call? The Baron had had plenty of time to hire him by now. I wanted to check the Baron's story with what he had told me. Just in case there was a chink.

The room seemed suffocatingly hot. I dried my face again and closed my eyes. I was in a steel box welded shut. The air was black cotton. It stank. Time was running out.

CHAPTER NINE

Night. Montrose Park and the patrolman under the street lamp. A young cop, tall and square-jawed. Some illusions left. Probably still straight. But the Park detail didn't offer much in the way of gravy. A few drops, maybe, but nothing tempting like the vice beat where the sauce was rich and highly spiced.

I was on my fourth cigarette and my mouth tasted like a laundry bag. A little longer and the cop would stroll over and suggest I move along. The time was nine twenty-three. I had been waiting for Megan nearly half an hour. At nine o'clock it had begun to bother me. That and the fact that the Baron had never gone to Artie's office or even called him. For a man with a problem as large as the Baron claimed, it was a perplexing study in indifference. No show. Neither the Baron nor Megan. For what reasons? Lucia Melho's death? That was the likely answer. Megan would know Lucia was dead if Kellaway's men had interrogated the Baron. She would assume I knew as well and the reason for meeting me would dissolve. She could have reasoned that way.

Or it could be something else.

The cop had stopped twirling his nightstick. He was looking at my car. I had been parked too long to suit him. He was making up his mind about me. I tossed my cigarette to the street, started the engine and pulled away from the curb. I could do without his writing my license number in his notebook.

Over R Street and past the Baron's lair. A dim light framed an upstairs window. The garage light showed the doors closed. The downstairs windows were dark. If I had had my wits about me earlier and gotten the phone number, I could have called Molly, traded Irish blarney with her and inquired about Miss Megan. I could have called Anita, too, but not to ask about her half-sister. All the call would have given me would have been another tryst, a chance to indulge in the tack-room games program. Another night, Anita. The corpse of an old woman lies chill and stiff in the mortuary cooler. Her murderer still lives. Another time, Anita, when death and lies are less in the air than tonight.

I fumbled in the glove compartment, pulled out the grog flask and nibbled a snort. Witches' Eve. A cadaverous moon and an arched-back cat on every fence. A night to prowl. Tabby the Cat. Goblins and werewolves. Graveyard lights. I shivered and put away the bottle. I was getting lightheaded. Light if you will this graying head but spare my alcohol, he said.

Jamming on the brakes, I wrenched the wheel savagely and headed back. At Avon Place I turned down, switched off the lights and parked half a block from the house where Al Welinsky had gone the night before. Two apartments on each of the two floors. Four possibilities. Was Al rooming off-campus or was the apartment just a place to sleep off a whisky breath? There was light in all of the windows. That meant light in Al's apartment, too. Possibly Al as well. I watched for ten minutes and then I got out of the Olds and walked up Avon to R and over to Montrose Park.

The patrolman was off on his run down Lovers Lane. I sat down on a sidewalk bench, lighted a cigarette and pulled down my hat brim. After a while the patrolman strolled back to the lamp, bit off a chew of tobacco and regarded me with unenthusiastic eyes. I dropped my butt, ground it into the sidewalk and crossed the street.

From there I went slowly past the library that Megan had used to cover our last night's meeting. I chewed another cigarette on the steps and went back toward the car.

As I was getting in I noticed a woman hurrying down Avon Place. A woman with hair light even in the darkness, high heels and a wrap-around polo coat. As she neared the apartment she slowed and turned in. Opening the hall door, she disappeared inside. Anita.

I pushed back my hat and scratched the side of my jaw. A snuggery, no less. Anita's. And the chauffeur had a key. That made her as exclusive as General Delivery. I wondered if Al were waiting for her, chilled drinks in tall glasses, or if Al would be along later when the chores were done.

The chauffeur and the Baroness. The Lady and the Tramp. The Tramp and the Tramp. Nice. Lovely. A nifty for the Baron to ponder. If he knew. I closed my eyes and leaned on the door handle. I could see her stepping out of her skirt, fluffing her hair, preening before a mirror, then slipping into something filmy and inviting. Molding a brandy snifter in her hands, sipping delicately while waiting for the click of a key in the door lock. It made quite a scene. It played beautifully. A natural. I opened my eyes to banish it and slid into my seat.

If I had felt less than noble last night the feeling was gone now, flushed away like garbage from a sink.

The front door opened and two people came out, a man and a woman. I peered at them as they passed under the street light but they were nobody I knew. Just tenants, probably, unaware of their good fortune in having rented in the same building as a member, by marriage, of the minor nobility.

There was nothing in that for me. Not even nostalgia. I pushed down my hat, started the engine and drove away.

I didn't care that Anita was playing house with the family chauffeur; it went true to form. What I didn't like was sharing her favors with someone else, particularly big Al Welinsky. A lovely, talented little bosco, Anita, with her toes still touching the gutter.

By the time I reached Massachusetts I had gotten her pretty well out of my mind—with a little help from Megan whose failure to meet me was still a puzzler. Lucia Melho's death could only have worsened Megan's problem; in theory, at least, she still needed help from someone. None would be forthcoming from big sister or her chauffeur-paramour, so that narrowed the availables down to me. And I was on my way home.

Overhead the branches formed a leafy vault above the Avenue. The moon peered through the branches as tentatively as a comeback actor looking for encores. The air was damp and warm. A poor night for sleeping—even without a troubled mind.

I fitted the Olds into its slot, checked the desk for mail and went on up to my apartment.

It was now about ten forty-five. A little early to hit the pads, a little late to do anything else. At the bar I constructed a sturdy highball, wandered over to the Ampex and laid on a stereo reel. Before I sat down on the sofa I took off my coat and shoes and loosened my tie. Sinking back on the cushions, I stared up at the shadowed ceiling and thought what a badly mishandled and fruitless day it had been. Me and Kellaway. The Baron and me. Artie and me. Garaldo and me. Me and nobody-but-who-should-have-been-Megan. And, finally, me alone.

It seemed eventually always to brew down to that. Dregs. That and no inspiration. Nothing but a sense of not having played it as smart as I should have if I had thought things through.

I sipped my drink. It was as husky as Al Welinsky looked but easier on the face. Much easier. I remembered him lying on the gravel drive and grinned. *You bend over to touch your toes and I'll show you where the Wild Goose goes.* If Al had any problems I couldn't imagine what they were. Three squares daily, a good salary and the use of the boss's wife on odd nights. A lot of fellows would settle for less and love it. I could think of times in my own life when it would have looked like Mohammedan heaven. Especially Korea. Where everybody is named Kim.

Sitting up I massaged my drink. The mixture looked cloudy. Stale ice cubes. As if that affected the taste. Or the purpose. I thought of Megan Dos Santos, her lovely girl's face and her stunning woman's body. Half-child, half-woman, and a past hidden behind a barrier as impenetrable as obsidian. I remembered her voice, the fullness of her lips and the taste of her mouth.

I thought about those things and I drank my drink and listened to light gay music and when both were finished I went off to bed.

⚜ ⚜ ⚜

Air Raid!

The gong was ringing, a big temple bell clanging wildly. I tried to run but my feet were rooted in mud. I was too weak to lift them. Cold sweat covered my throat. The bell clanged a nightmare tattoo and my eyes searched the black sky....

The dream still gripped me as I sat up and snatched at the telephone. The demoniac ringing stopped. I could hear my breath in my throat as I husked. "Yeah. Who's calling?"

"Steve—it's me, can you—"

"Who? Oh, you, Megan. Where the hell were you tonight?"

"I can't explain now. You've got to come here. Please come at once."

My feet hit the cold floor with a shattering jar. "Where are you?"

"Home. R Street."

"What is it? If you're in danger I'll call the police."

"God, no," her voice shuddered. "Not the police. Just come."

The line went dead.

Under my pajamas hair prickled as though a magnet were stroking me. Switching on the light I stripped, dressed and laced on my Walther. The time was two-fourteen. Swearing I raced for the elevator, dived into the Olds and roared out of the garage, headed for R Street. I broke six traffic laws getting there, but I made it in close to ten minutes, parked in the shadows and began walking toward the big front gate.

The plainclothes car was gone. If the police still had the house under surveillance the men were well concealed. The front gate was open. So was one garage door. The Delahaye was gone.

I ran up the sidewalk, took the porch steps in threes and pounded on the door. It opened inward and I saw Molly's stark face. Wordlessly she pointed toward the living room and I brushed through the drapes.

The crystal chandelier glowed with a thousand yellow-blue flames. The tall chairs cast shadows as long as gallows and standing beside the half-opened study doors was Megan Dos Santos.

She wore a dressing gown of dark blue silk, caught around the waist by a tasseled silk belt. There were feathery things on her feet and one open hand made a V at her throat. The other hand opened and closed as she breathed. Her face was as white as bleached bone.

Her shoulders slumped and she seemed to sag forward. I caught her and felt her arms go around me. "Thank you," she whispered. "Oh, thank you for coming." Then her full weight was against me. She had fainted but she was too young to have it last long.

As I stood there holding her, I looked through the partly opened doors of the study and saw that a light near the desk was on. It was the only light in the dark room.

Behind the desk was a chair and the chair held a man. It held only part of his weight because the upper part of his body was pressing down against the desk. The light was behind him and from where I stood he looked as though he were sleeping. I could see only the top of his head, the fingers of one hand.

Consciousness flowed back into Megan's body. Her knees stiffened and she stood away. One hand brushed back her hair and she said, "I'm sorry. I'll be all right now." Molly was beside her, stroking her arms, massaging her wrists. I straightened my shoulders and walked through the sliding doors.

Beside the door frame there was a wall switch. I snapped it on and went up to the desk and stopped.

The man's coat was dark blue cheviot, his silver-gray hair lay smoothly against the top of his skull. From where I stood I could see part of the right side of his face, no more. Slightly above the place where the jawbone joined there was a large blue-black hole fringed with powder punctures. The man was Baron Alejandro Esquivel and he was very very dead.

The gun that had caused his death lay near the fingertips of his right hand. It was a flintlock pistol with a checkered saw-handle, heavy octagonal barrel and no ornamentation. I had seen the pistol before—or its mate. Half-kneeling I read the engraving on the top of the barrel: *Jos. Manton 1818.* Nothing more. I stood up and looked around for the mate. It lay in its lined case near the corner of the antique gilt escritoire, sleekly evil.

Turning, I called to Megan, "Have you touched anything?"

"No. I don't think I did. I don't remember."

"Pull yourself together," I said sharply, "the Baron's dead."

"I heard the shot. It woke me and I came down. I found him like this." Her voice was steady now, calmer. A dry-eyed voice. She had had her faint and now it was behind her.

I turned back to the corpse and looked at the study's single window. It was open a few inches as though for ventilation.

Behind me Megan said, "You will call the police now?"

"It might look better if you did. And it might be much better if the police never learned I came here."

"What will they do?"

"They'll do everything you might expect them to do, and more. A great deal more. Why did you call me first?"

"I—I didn't know what else to do. I was afraid. I thought they might think I killed him."

"Why?"

Her face was like chiseled stone. "He was a devil. I hated him."

"Enough to kill him?"

"Enough to kill him a hundred times."

"I wouldn't go quite that far with the police."

"It is true."

I glanced down at the slumped torso. "He could have killed himself."

Her head moved slowly, negatively. Then she glided toward me, around the end of the table and past the end of a wall bookcase. Her hand lifted and she pointed to a round black cavity in the wall not more than a foot in diameter. A heavy stepped door hung outward on its hinges. There was a combination dial in the center of the door.

She said, "The pearls are gone."

"That changes things," I said. "Is there anything else I ought to know? Where's Anita?"

Her eyebrows lifted. I said, "I mean the Baroness."

A small cynical smile played over her lips. Moving toward me she said, "I thought perhaps you might know. She left here at ten o'clock. No one has seen her since then."

"Did you look in her room?"

"I did that," Molly said. "The bed was turned down but nobody has lain in it this night."

Megan said, "That is also why I called you. The police will want to know where Anita was when Alejandro died. I thought we might wait to call them until she—"

"Until she stumbles home?" I shook my head. "Not very practical. Where did she say she was going—or didn't she bother?"

Megan looked at Molly. Molly shrugged. "A movie, she said. But if you ask me—"

"They'll ask you, never fear. And the bobbies here aren't noted for chivalry toward ladies." I turned back to Megan. "Where's Wells?"

"With Anita—I imagine," she said lazily. "Or didn't you know?"

"I read it in a gypsy teacup. Well, they can alibi each other. The big car's not in the garage, by the way."

Megan said nothing. Behind her smoky eyes pressure seemed to be building up. But her face was as blank as desert sand. Too blank. She ought to be talking now, words coming in a rush. Instead there was nothing. She breathed deeply, her breasts lifted and suddenly she smiled. "There's nothing to do but call the police, is there?"

I shook my head. Thinking of the hard times ahead for her I was fresh out of throw-away lines. There was the sound of a key in the front-door lock. We turned as the door opened and Anita stepped in.

She stopped uncertainly, the key dangling from its chain, closed the door slowly and stared at us blearily. She was drunk.

I broke the frozen silence. "Hello, Big Sister. We were wondering when you'd stop in."

CHAPTER TEN

Mid-morning in my office. Artie beside my desk, a cigarette dangling from his lips. He shook his head slowly and said, "The Baron's one client I'm just as glad didn't drop by. Much less hire me."

I tapped a pencil against an upper tooth and yawned. What sleep I had managed to get had been only a bailing can against a sea of fatigue. I blinked and rubbed my eyes.

Artie said, "What happened when the widow came home? Fried, you say?"

"Crisp around the edges. It wasn't what you'd call a pretty scene. One look at what was left of Alejandro and she caught the screaming fantods. When she saw the empty safe she doubled it and added brass."

Artie chuckled. "Funny how money affects the ladies—particularly the loyal, grieving widows. And how they cuss the dear departed when they find out Daddy didn't leave a bundle in the bank."

I pointed the pencil at my phone. "Sometime today Kellaway's going to call me up and tell me the Baron is dead. He'll sneer a little and laugh like hell because I wasn't in on it."

"You gonna tell him?"

"Why spoil his fun?" I yawned. This time I didn't bother to cover my mouth. Artie winced. "You got a breath like a musty cellar."

"It could be liquor. There was some tippling done last night. And not all by the Baron's widow."

"Where was she when the deed was done?"

"She was still in hysterics when I left. It seemed to sober her but not enough. By then the police were on their way. She may have told them, but I doubt it."

"What about the kid—the sister?"

I looked at my watch. "We're lunching at one."

"I see," Artie said archly. "The way you describe her she oughta look sensational in black."

"She'd look sensational in a Mother Hubbard trimmed with moldy canvas."

Artie raised one eyebrow. "She's only nineteen."

"That's legal," I said. "Any arguments?"

He shrugged. "This reminds me of the Calvo girls, a while back. One sister's never quite enough for you. You gotta get to know the whole family."

I let it slide by. "Hod Gurney's representing the widow and Megan. I got that taken care of before I turned in."

"I didn't know Hod handled criminal cases."

"Who says it's a criminal case?"

He sat forward and stared at me. "It's murder, Steve. That makes it a criminal case."

"For the murderer it does. But the murderer doesn't have to be Anita or Megan."

He snorted. "Who you figure done it?"

I stared up at the ceiling. "At the moment I don't find myself caring a hell of a lot. It's a little tough on the Baron but from the beginning he looked like gallows-meat."

Artie shivered. "I like the way you put that: tough. Yeah, I'd call it tough, all right. Tough enough. What about the pearls?"

I looked down from the ceiling. "I have a feeling they'll turn up. Not tomorrow maybe, but in time."

"Why?" he said sharply.

I shrugged and put down my pencil. "In the first place they're not readily negotiable. As I understand it the string is close to unique. As the owner the Baron could have sold them but the killer can't. Right now I'm wondering why they were even taken."

"Hell," Artie said. "The killer had to murder the Baron to get the pearls."

I studied a fly marching slowly across the base of my pen set. When he had reached the pen barrel, I said, "When I trooped in there last night it looked like suicide. You can't take fingerprints from a checkered grip, but the pistol lay in a believable place, the body position was about right and the entrance wound was what you'd expect: heavy flash burn and plenty of impacted powder grains. Without any contrary evidence it could have gone down as suicide. The open safe makes the difference."

"The Baron could have opened the safe himself and put the pearls someplace else."

"And then sat down and cocked the flintlock?" I shook my head. "He loved those pearls, Artie. If his story was even partly true he was afraid they might be stolen."

"Then why didn't he come over to my office and hire me?"

I lifted my eyes heavenward. "It'll take a spiritualist to get the answer to that. And a suicide guy isn't a guy who calls the police and asks to have his life protected either. Puff on that for a while."

"I will," Artie said as he stood up. "Sometime when I'm getting paid for it. Or am I still working for you?"

"You are. I want to know which of the four apartments on Avon Place is the love nest."

"Want Garaldo covered?"

I nodded. "If your boys need a friend inside the Bedford the bell captain has the unlikely name of Chester. I want to know if Macaluso visits him again. Or Al Welinsky. And where Macaluso hangs out."

Artie turned and walked toward the door. He put his hand on the knob and looked back. "I still don't get it. What's in this for you?"

"A girl," I said dreamily.

"Or two?" he leered.

"Or none," I snapped.

He opened the door and said, "Once I got lucky and won a pass to a Turkish bath. Trouble was the bath was in Turkey."

I slammed a folded newspaper at him, he ducked out of the door and it closed behind him. After a while I got up, picked up the newspaper and dropped it in the waste basket. The Baron's murder had been too late for the first editions but it ought to be on the street about now. Kellaway hadn't called. He was probably savoring the situation and holding off as long as possible for the big guffaw. I wondered how he would like it when he learned that Anita was Al Welinsky's doxy. It was the kind of basic motivation policemen loved. But in this case the pair was probably bedded down in the Avon Place snuggery when the Baron stepped off. I thought about the death of Lucia Melho the night before and wondered what it had to do with the Baron's murder. Write it off as coincidence or make something out of it. And to do that might be harder than it looked. A lot harder. Unless one of the persons concerned decided to talk: either Anita or Megan. And they might not care to talk, either of them.

I wondered if the Baron had left a will and whether it had been found. I wondered who had taken the Maracaibo pearls and whether they would ever be found. They were questions that needed answers. Someone knew what the answers were. At least one person and probably more.

Glancing at my wrist watch I realized that it was after eleven o'clock. So far today I had done no work for any of my clients. Megan was meeting me at one, giving me less than two hours to try to turn out some work.

I sat down behind the desk and began shuffling papers, looking for something that could be solved by one o'clock. Only I never got the chance. The door opened and Captain Kellaway came in. There was a shredded cigar clamped between his teeth and his hat looked glued onto his head. He sat down, folded a leg over a chair arm and said, "Tell me you didn't know the Baron was killed last night."

"You're writing the dialogue."

He grunted. "I figured as much. Gurney was on the job a little too fast for happenstance."

I picked up my pipe, filled the bowl and lighted it. When it was drawing well I said, "I neglected to compliment you on the great job your boys did."

His eyes narrowed. "What great job?"

"Protecting the Baron's life."

Kellaway yanked the cigar from his mouth, swore and tossed it into the waste basket. "I had to pull them off at eight last night and send them over to cover a senator's house. That's the kind of luck I get."

"Don't fret over it. The Baron was ready for the big jump, anyway. Last night, tonight, next week. It was only a question of time."

Kellaway uncocked his knee and dropped his foot to the floor. "That's an interesting observation," he said quietly. "Care to expand on it?"

"It was only an observation," I murmured. "Fruit of an inventive mind."

"I wish I were sure of that." He stroked the night's growth of beard and stared at the Venetian blinds. "Well, the ladies are free on bond, you'll be glad to know."

"Have fun bullying them?"

"Sure. We stick them in an Iron Maiden and squeeze until the juice runs." He gazed at me disgustedly. "You know me: Kellaway, the Human Beast."

I reached into the desk drawer and pulled out a bottle of seven-year-old. Handing it to him I said, "I'll promise not to tell."

He unscrewed the cap, tilted the bottle and let about four ounces trickle down his throat. Mopping his mouth on a handkerchief, he handed back the pint. What little was left of it. Then he took a deep breath and sagged back against the chair cushion. After a while he opened his eyes. "The hours I keep I might as well be an obstetrician."

"Pay's better, too. And you'd be a hero to the ladies."

He took off his hat and balanced it on the chair arm. His forehead was dotted with perspiration. The way spring was taking hold it would be one hell of a sultry summer.

Pulling a fresh cigar from his coat pocket, he bit off the end and lighted it. Then he said, "I'd describe the death scene to you except I got the feeling you got it memorized already."

I let it pass.

"A plausible suicide," Kellaway said, "except for the theft of those damn pearls. How do you figure the killer opened the safe?"

"The Baron could have opened the safe to take out the pearls and gloat over them. Enter the killer. End of scene."

He shook his head and his mouth twisted. "I don't like it. That way it's an inside job. The window behind him was open."

"Any footprints outside the window?"

"There's a flagstone patio under the window," he said sourly. "So much for that."

"How many years has it been since anyone was killed by a flintlock?"

"The records don't go back that far. Apparently one of the pair killed the hero of Waterloo, the Iron Duke."

"So the legend goes."

He twisted the cigar slowly and said, "I wonder why the other pistol was loaded."

I leaned forward. "It was?"

He nodded.

"Maybe he was getting ready for a duel."

Kellaway snorted. "According to the widow he kept only one pistol of each pair loaded. That being the case why load the second pistol?"

"Maybe someone else loaded it."

"Who?"

"The killer."

He shook his head, stirring the cloud of thin blue smoke. "We'll let that weather a while and turn to the basic question: who wanted the Baron out of the way? Who would have had reason to kill him?"

"You've asked the ladies of the family?"

"You bet your life we have. The way they tell it he was a charming, lovable fellow without an enemy in the world." He pointed his cigar at me. "I don't believe it. Someone hated his guts. Who?"

I knocked some ash from my pipe and lighted it again. "In the course of previous conversations I mentioned a hood named Ducky Macaluso. You do anything about him?"

"We got the call out, but nothing yet."

"Where was the chauffeur last night?"

His eyes glinted slightly. "Off with Madame la Baroness. And both of them say the same. Would you know anything different?"

"They were doing what?"

He took out his cigar, leaned forward and dropped ash into the ash stand. "Over in Virginia at a drive-in movie. An old flic—one they could have seen months ago. Proving nothing at all. No ticket stubs because the drive-in don't give them."

I wasn't ready to tell him about the Avon Place love nest. Not yet. Not until I had a chance to talk with Megan. I sucked my pipe and managed to look bored with the whole thing. After a while Kellaway shrugged, put on his hat and stood up. "You've been a world of help," he said stonily. "Remind me to waste a lot of time here again."

"My time is yours. How goes the war on bookies, numbers runners and other enemies of society?"

"About like you'd expect." His lips made an indelicate sound and he went out of the office.

I put aside my pipe, listened to my arteries harden and went down to the barber shop for a shave. After that I drove over to Maine Avenue. Parking in the Yacht Club lot, I went in to the bar and ordered a whisky sour.

There was a lot of sun on the channel. It was slack tide and the boats lay idle at their moorings, my ketch among them. Sitting at the bar, I scribbled a note to myself to replace the starboard running light and finished my drink. An attendant came up to me and said, "Mistah Bentley, lady waiting for you in the clubrooms."

I gave him a quarter, slid down from the stool and walked up the stairs to the lounge.

She was sitting near the big observation window, a chic hat perched on the crown of her head. There were white gloves on her hands and she was wearing a dress of olive watered silk.

When she saw me she smiled and stood up. We moved over to a lounge away from the window glare, sat down and ordered champagne cocktails. I offered her a cigarette and lighted it. Then she leaned back comfortably, turned to me and said, "I think everything's going to be all right."

CHAPTER ELEVEN

"Let's hope so." I lighted a cigarette for myself, centered an ash tray on the cocktail table and looked at her. Her face showed only the slightest trace of fatigue and strain.

I said, "I've talked with Captain Kellaway. Evidently Hod Gurney did what he was supposed to do."

She nodded. "He was wonderful. I'm so glad you thought to call him."

The waiter delivered our drinks and said, "Call for you, Mr. Bentley."

I grimaced, lifted my glass and touched the rim to hers. She said, "What should we drink to?"

"A new life?"

"A new life."

I sipped, put down my glass and stood up. "No mourning, Megan? No tears for the Baron?"

She looked up at me and her eyes were steady. "I can't pretend what I don't feel."

I went over to the other side of the room and got into the booth. The voice was Artie's. He said, "Two things, Steve."

"Shoot."

"When Lucia Melho bought that house she paid for it in cash. The real-estate agent remembered because cash deals in that part of town happen once in twenty years. No checks, no bank drafts, just green money. Close to five thousand dollars."

"Interesting," I said. "Go on."

"According to Chester over at the Bedford our friend Garaldo checked out early this morning."

I swore. "He went where?"

"There was a plane ticket in his hand when he checked out. Chester talked to the cabbie afterward and it seems he drove Garaldo over the river to the airport. What do you make of that?"

"The same as you."

"That's what I was thinking."

"Any trace of Macaluso?"

"Not yet. You staying there a while?"

"Probably."

"I'll call if I get anything more."

Stepping out of the booth, I went back to Megan and sat down. There was a distant look in her eyes. Whatever else they held, fear was gone. "Business?" she asked.

I picked up my glass, admired the brittle stem and said, "I haven't done much about business the past few days."

"It's my fault," she said contritely, and laid one hand on my arm. "I'm truly sorry, Steve."

"It's not important. Suppose you tell me why you didn't meet me last night?"

"Alejandro forbade me to leave."

"Why?"

"He was in a strange mood—half-furious, half-frightened. I don't think he wanted to be left alone."

"You knew Lucia was dead?"

Her face sobered. "Alejandro told me, showed it to me in the paper. The news pleased him."

"For what reason?"

"It spared him paying her more money—he sent money to her every month, you know. I told you that before."

"You still haven't told me what she was keeping for you."

Her fingers twirled the stem delicately. She glanced out over the water and said, "It had to do with Alejandro. Now it isn't important."

"Where is it now?"

"I think it must have been destroyed."

"Why would you think that, Megan?"

"Because I think Alejandro took it when he killed her."

I stared at her then I set down my glass. It was a sneak punch, as unexpected as a *banzai* raid. Calmly she said, "Lucia had no other enemies."

"He killed her to stop paying retirement money—or to get whatever it was that she was keeping for you?"

Megan took a deep breath. "Really, Steve, it doesn't matter now. I'm sorry about Lucia, but the man who murdered her is dead." She lifted her pocketbook from the sofa to the cocktail table. Then she turned, to me and said, "I've lived with it too long. I don't want to think about it anymore."

I finished my drink and signaled for two more.

She was gazing at me across the rim of her glass, her face held a kittenish, provocative expression. "Don't think I'm cold and callous, Steve. I'm not."

I shrugged. "Let's change the subject. Where did you learn to speak such remarkably good English?"

"In schools. In Switzerland, Italy and Portugal. And briefly in England."

"Once you told me Anita was a high-class whore and Alejandro a thief."

She nodded slightly. "Alejandro used Anita in his business deals. She was, shall we say, a lure. To me she was and is a whore even though Anita told me they were married."

"Did you believe it?"

One hand tightened. "I wanted to. I was only a child then and it was necessary to me to believe that they were man and wife. Now it's less important."

"Did the Baron ever make a will?"

Her lips grew bitter. "He made a will once. A long time ago. If I married before his death I was to receive nothing."

"An unusual stipulation."

"He was an unusual man," she said in a voice clotted with hate.

The new drinks arrived. The waiter polished the table and took away the empty glasses. I said, "Among the men whom Alejandro defrauded was one a man named Mario Garaldo?"

Her eyebrows lifted. "How did you know that?"

"He's here in Washington. Or was until he checked out of his hotel early this morning."

"Do the police know Mario was here?"

"I don't think so."

"Is it necessary that you tell them?"

"Not entirely."

Her hand slid down my arm and covered my palm. "Then I would prefer that nothing be said. Of course, Anita might know he was here."

"Why?"

She shrugged. "Alejandro pushed her into Mario's arms. I think he fell in love with her. One night I heard a terrible scene between Alejandro and Anita and she threatened to leave him and go to Mario. She said Mario loved her."

"Nice people," I said, drinking deeply. "I think you're all perfectly lovely."

Her face froze. She drew away from me and said, "You Americans—so safe, so comfortable. So sure of yourselves. What can you know of our Civil War, of our terrible poverty? Of what it is to starve, to send a daughter to the streets to bring back money for a little bread? In Europe that has happened everywhere. Only here have you been spared. And you should thank God for it."

I took her hand between mine. "I'm sorry," I said. "Smugness is a national curse. You won't hear that from me again."

She lifted my hands and her lips brushed the back of my hand. "We are another race," she said huskily. "Another people. What can we have in common with you?"

I felt my throat tighten. I was the heavy-handed American, as subtle as a shovel. People were turning to look at us. I lowered my hands and picked up my glass. When I looked at her again, her eyes were misty. I said, "We might have a little lunch now and row out to my boat afterward."

"Which one is yours?"

I pointed it out to her.

"It's a beautiful boat, Steve. Do you sail very much?"

"As much as I can. Weekends mostly."

"I learned to sail on Lake Lucerne. It was a lovely lake. A lovely time of my life." Her face shadowed and she looked down at the golden champagne. I called the waiter over, we ordered lobster salad and ate on the terrace.

After that I got a bottle of champagne and a cooler, helped Megan into the dory and rowed out to my ketch.

While I was icing the champagne, she went below. After a while she came up, without her gloves or purse and barefoot. We lay around the cockpit on cushions, sunning lazily until the champagne was gone and then I rowed back to the dock.

I tucked her into the Olds, and as I turned onto Maine Avenue I said, "What are your plans now? Yours and Anita's?"

"I don't know yet. It's too soon to make plans. And there's the problem of money."

"I thought Alejandro had plenty of it."

"He did. Most of it is still in Switzerland. In those secret numbered accounts. Unless we can find the records we may never get the money."

"You'll sell the house, won't you?"

She shrugged. "I suppose Anita will. The house is not paid for. Alejandro paid some money to get possession, but not a large amount. So there is that problem. But the larger problem is whether Anita will be recognized as his widow. If that happens she will inherit whatever Alejandro left."

"Including the pearls."

"If they are ever found." She turned to me. "I want to leave that horrible house, Steve. I can't live there any longer."

I nodded.

"This afternoon I'm moving to a hotel. After that I want to take an apartment. Perhaps you could help me find one?"

"Of course."

"Not an expensive place. Not until we know about the money."

"That's sensible. Can I take you to the hotel?"

"Please don't. You're neglecting your business dreadfully. Molly can help me."

"And you'll let me know where you are?"

The pressure of her hand answered me.

I drove around the Tidal Basin, past Watergate and the *Titanic* Memorial where we had parked two nights before. Where she had kissed me. Then along to the Parkway and up into Georgetown.

The driveway's iron gate was open and the Delahaye was in its stall. A patrolman sat on the front porch playing handies with his nightstick. An old harness bull on pasture detail. Nothing to do but let the sergeant know who came and went. And when.

Opening the car door for her, I said, "Call me if there's anything I can do. Or Hod Gurney."

"I'd much rather call you," she said quietly, leaned over and kissed me. I put my arms around her and drew her close. The harness bull stopped playing handies, sat upright and goggled at us. I closed my eyes and kissed her again. It could have been the champagne or the spring season, but I could have gone on kissing her for a long time. Until nightfall, at least. And after that.

Finally she drew away, dabbed my lips with a tiny handkerchief to erase the lipstick and said, "I've had a wonderful time, darling. Thank you so much."

She stepped down onto the drive, crossed the grass border and walked toward the front steps. High heels, trim ankles and long tapered thighs. At the steps she turned and waved at me. I waved and backed down the drive.

Al Welinsky came out of the garage and stared at me. He was wearing a mechanic's jumper stained with grease. He wiped his hands on a belt rag and made an obscene gesture. I kept on backing until my wheels hit R Street. Then I turned and drove back to the office.

From my desk I called Kellaway but the sergeant said he was off duty. Home asleep, probably. I wanted to pass along part of what Megan had told me, but it could wait. It was history now. The parties concerned were dead.

The sun and champagne had filled my head with glass wool. All I was good for was a couple of signatures. Then I went out to the john and soaked my head in icy water. When I dragged back into the office, Mrs. Bross gave me a pruny look that spoke volumes and handed me a telephone number. "A young lady just called. She was very anxious to have you call back."

"Name?"

"She left none," she sniffed, "but from her voice it seemed to be a matter of life and death."

I carried the number back to my office, shut the door and dialed.

The voice that answered was low and huskily urgent. It was the voice of a woman in deadly fear. Anita.

"Steve," she whispered, and ice coated my vertebrae, "come to me at once. *Please* do this for me."

I gripped the phone. "Where are you? Home?"

"No. On Avon Place. A white house," she gave me the street number and repeated it. "An apartment on the first floor. Number two."

"Look," I said, "can't you tell me—?" but the phone clicked down. Hard. I stood up and replaced the phone. I knew the place, all right. It was the love nest address. The place where she had gotten soused last night with Al the chauffeur. There wasn't time to get my Olds out of the garage so I flagged a cab and we sped across to Georgetown. The tall elms shadowed the quiet streets. House shutters were closed and the air was as drowsy as a Louisiana bayou. I had a dollar ready and when the taxi slowed I dropped it on the front seat, pushed the door open and jumped to the street. Running up the walk I remembered my Walther hanging in my closet instead of under my arm but I didn't dwell on it. The entrance door was open. I went into the dark hall, ran to the end and pounded on the door.

It opened and I saw Anita standing in the room. The back of one hand was pressed across her mouth, her eyes wide with terror. She was standing too far from the door to have opened it, but the thought came to me too late. Much too late. By then I had taken two steps into the room, the hand snapped suddenly from her mouth and she screamed.

Something caught the back of my head. Pain blinded me. I felt my knees give way and her scream faded like a dying siren.

Then, only blackness.

CHAPTER TWELVE

Consciousness returned, a millimeter at a time. A roaring as dull and distant as a jungle river swelled and faded off into silence. Then the throb of blood pumping hard through flaccid arteries, a fast urgent rhythm that turned into pain. I had dropped into a deep well, head first, and now I was climbing up the rocky wall. A flash of light. More pain. A sense of pressure. I moved one leg. It drew up, flexed and turned. The roaring came back.

I rested. The roaring went away.

My eyes opened. They stared at a dust-green ceiling. The corner lamp cast a round shadow where the ceiling and the walls joined. I pried myself up on an elbow and looked around. I had glimpsed the room briefly before I was sapped; now it was mine to examine. I was alone.

Varnished maple furniture, the kind that sells to engaged working couples. A modernistic corner lamp. Passion-pink walls and a square mirror near the door. I sat up. The sofa was near. I crawled to it and rested. The effort shot wild flashes of color through my eyeballs. The back of my head was hard and swollen and painful. I touched the hair tenderly and felt something rough and caked. I took my hand away. I knew what it was.

On the end table stood an open bottle of Canadian Club. I reached for it, tilted and swallowed. Coughing and choking, I wiped my mouth and set the bottle down. When the liquor hit my stomach I stood up, swaying, holding on to the sofa arm. I was dizzy and sick.

"Anita," I croaked, but the word echoed emptily through the room.

The blinds were drawn. I staggered to the window and peered outside. There was barely enough light to make out the house next door. I had been a long time asleep. And the way my head felt I was lucky to have come out of it at all.

An open door leading into a white enameled kitchenette showed a stove, the corner of a refrigerator, a chair and a table. Another door leading into a bedroom. A dresser and the footboard of a low bed. Beyond, deep shadows. Nothingness.

My stomach gurgled and tried to jump up my throat but I gulped air and forced it down. Gritting my teeth in pain I stumbled toward the bedroom door, reached the frame and felt for the light switch. White light flooded the little room.

On the far wall a bathroom door with a negligee hanging from the inside hook. On the dresser a lucite brush and comb set and a bottle of toilet water. From the bed the buzzing of flies.

A woman lay back on the bed. A naked woman whose eyes stared unblinkingly at the ceiling light. Naked but for her high-heeled shoes which rested flat on the floor. The backs of her naked thighs were flattened under her weight. Her hair was ice-blond and she could have been resting except for the contorted grimace on her face, the bulging eyes and the tongue that had been bitten through.

Around her throat a black belt had been drawn tight and knotted. But for the leather's smooth sheen it might have been a black tie. I stared at it, felt my waist and giggled. My belt. Then I felt my stomach rise. I vaulted around the edge of the bed and vomited in the toilet. When the spasm stopped I shook myself, turned on the tap and splashed my face. Rinsing my mouth, I dried myself, toweled the tap handle and replaced the towel. On the tile floor stood a pair of feathery heeled slippers. I went back into the bedroom.

Her clothes were draped over the back of the room's only chair. Killed first and peeled like an animal. I shivered. Flies covered her tongue like sequins but Anita Esquivel was beyond caring.

The man who had killed her had set me up as the patsy. My belt bound her throat. I thought about taking it off but it was an ordinary three-dollar belt, used and untraceable. My final gift to her. Some gift, Bentley.

I saw the staring eyes, the rigid death grimace and the beautifully sculptured body, now white clay. Then I turned and left the room. With my handkerchief I polished the Canadian Club bottle, set it down and went into the kitchen. Covering my fingers with my handkerchief I opened the rear door and stepped outside. From the railed porch three board steps led to the alley. I walked quietly out to Avon Place, turned and followed it around to 30th Street. Without the belt my pants felt loose. I tried not to remember where the belt was.

Morgan Pharmacy at P Street. Four aspirins and a glass of water. On an empty stomach the aspirin ought to take hold. The pain had localized now. It felt like an angry scalp carbuncle that needed lancing. I felt weak and confused. I stepped into the phone booth and called Kellaway. Still off duty. Would Lieutenant Wolcott do? No, he would not. I hung up and peered out of the booth. A lad in chino pants and a Princeton cut was scanning the want ad notices on the neighborhood bulletin board. A friendly place. I used another dime and called the Seventh precinct. "Avon Place," I said. "The white apartment building near the corner. I heard screams on the first floor. Apartment two."

"Drunks, maybe," a voice drawled.

"Go see for yourself," I snarled and hung up.

Opening the door, I tottered out. My collar was hot and limp with sweat. I wondered why the killer hadn't tipped the cops. I must have been out close to two hours. My belt around her neck; me on the floor. A frame, but not well done. An empty trap.

Dusk on the street. I flagged a passing cab and rode it out to my apartment.

I didn't want anyone waiting by the door. I didn't want anyone inside waiting in the darkness with a gun. I pushed through the door and flashed on the light. Nothing. I shivered. Nerves.

A long pull from the nearest bottle, then a hot shower and two more aspirin. I felt a little giddy but the pain was subsiding. My stomach was purged, I needed food. When I was dry and dressed again, I swallowed a pint of milk. I was wearing another belt, brown alligator this time.

The door buzzer rang.

I went to the closet and pulled down my P-38, slid a shell in the chamber and walked to the door. The killer could have seen me leave Avon Place before the cops arrived. He could be on the other side of the door now, ready to finish me off. I flattened against the wall and opened the door. A man stood in the dark corridor.

"Slow," I said. "Enter easy."

"Put it away," Kellaway drawled. "Every punk with a pistol permit wants to play copper." He came in and kicked the door shut.

I clicked the pistol on safe and laid it on a table.

"That's better," Kellaway said. "Why the special measures? Jumpy or something?"

"Or something. You still off duty?"

"Why?"

"There's a drink for the making."

"I'll do that little thing." He walked over to the bar, dropped cubes in a glass, laced them with liquor and carried his glass back. He sat down. He was shaved and the circles under his eyes were lighter. Dropping his hat over my gun, he drank from his glass and stared at me moodily. "How you been, boy?" he said finally.

"I've been better. Sleep do you some good?"

"Plenty. But they woke me up."

"Not very considerate."

He shrugged. "Police business. The bitter with the better. How'd you know I was turned in?"

"I called a few times."

His eyebrows lifted. "Concerning which, Stevie?"

I picked up a cigarette and lighted it. Inhaling I took the cigarette away and stubbed it out. It tasted like a dust bin. "Various matters," I said.

"Anything important?"

"The last time I called they offered me Wolcott instead. You know Wolcott.

"A smart boy. You don't like him?"

"One of the college kids. An educated cop. How many beats has he ever patrolled? What's he know about tough guys in dark alleys and little junkies with big guns?" I shrugged. "What's all the delicate fencing about? You didn't brush by just to pilfer the fruit stand."

He drank the rest of his scotch and set the glass down. "How right you are. You being so close to the Esquivel family I thought you'd want to be among the first to know."

I said nothing.

He pulled a dime cigar from his pocket, nicked the end with a thumbnail and lighted it. Gazing up at me through a wraith of smoke he said, "Within the last hour the Seventh Precinct got a call from a fellow complaining about noise in an apartment on Avon Place. Screams, the fellow said. So the prowlies beetle over and the apartment door's locked. So they come in the kitchen door." He inhaled and blew a dragon blast across the room. "Whaddaya know. There's a dame in the bedroom. Naked as September Morn and deader than burlesque." He peered up at me. "A man's black belt around her throat. So they roust me out of bed and ride me crosstown to look at the stiff, and ..." His voice trailed off. "You tell me," he rasped.

"Anita Esquivel," I said and walked over to the bar.

"One hundred per cent correct!"

I mixed a fresh drink for myself and leaned back against the bar. He was sitting forward, both hands clenched into fists on his knees. "You must be psychic," he sneered.

I shook my head. "I was the guy who called the Seventh Precinct. I was there. The belt was mine."

His fist hit the table edge and the glassware jumped. "Thanks a million! That's the easiest confession today as well as being the first. Now, just how did your belt get twined around her ivory throat?"

I told him.

When I had finished he got up, strolled over to the bar and trickled more liquor into his glass. Then he came back, tilted the lampshade and shone the light on the back of my head.

"You'll live," he muttered. "How's it feel?"

"The way it always does."

"Figure a man sapped you?"

"I never heard of a female killer who'd strip a woman's corpse and leave it naked."

"That's because you haven't got twenty-six years of police work under your belt." He choked off the last word and looked guilty. "Anyway, that's a watery theory. You know, I'm pretty sore at you."

"That's standard."

"The only reason you didn't call my house was out of consideration?"

"Plus the fact that the lady was dead and the killer already had about a two-hour start."

He put down his glass, jarred ash from his cigar and said, "I'll accept that. Now, why did she call you to come to the apartment?"

"So someone could slug me."

He made a wry face. "What for?"

"To frame me for a killing that hadn't yet taken place. He used my belt, didn't he? Left me lying there."

"But he didn't tip the police. That's where that one drifts away. I like it she was scared and wanted company. But before you got there the killer had taken over."

"Maybe," I said. "Only I don't see it making a hell of a lot of difference."

"Only this: whether you were lured there by the killer or whether he didn't expect you."

I put my elbows on my knees and ran my hands through my hair. I was weak and tired. There was too much liquor in my guts, too much death in my nostrils. I said, "Have it any way you want."

Breath whistled in his throat. "I could use a little help from you, Steve."

I took away my hands and sat up again. I licked my lips and said, "Earlier today I spent a couple of hours with Anita's half-sister, Megan. One reason I tried to get you was to tell you what she said about Lucia Melho's murder."

"Murder number one."

"Megan thinks the Baron killed her."

"So do I." He leaned forward and gave me a crocodile smile. "The boys picked up a little piece of evidence when they shook the place down. Not enough for a conviction, but with the Baron dead we don't have to try."

"What kind of evidence?"

"A little tie clasp with an engraved crest on it. Looked like silver at first but it turned out to be platinum. It was on the floor."

"How did you connect it with him?"

He smiled. "We showed it to the widow earlier today, let her think it was part of the stuff we took off him when we stripped the Baron's body." He lifted his glass and sipped iced scotch. "So much for that one. That leaves us with two left. Who killed the Baron? Who killed his lady?"

I said, "I'll give it some thought. After my head shrinks down to size."

"Poor boy," he said unctuously. "One must pay a price if one meddles in police affairs." He set down his glass and stood up. "Why not drop over to Horror House and break the news to kid sister?"

"That's the sort of stuff you get paid to do."

"Go ahead," he urged. "You're the suave, polished type. Coming from you it would listen easier."

I looked up at him. "It was kind of a complex family. What it lacked mainly was affection."

"Go on, call her."

I gazed at him wearily. "Megan doesn't live there anymore. She moved out this afternoon."

His mouth clicked shut like a spring. "And she didn't bother to tell anyone where she was going. Laddie, we got a drag out for her right now."

I got to my feet. "Great," I said sourly. "That shows a lot of deep thought and professional foresight. The kid moves to a hotel so you slap her name on the fugitive list. Would you mind telling me why?"

He scooped his hat from the table and spun the pistol around. "It was a family of three," he said. "A family with a lot of dough at its disposal. Plus a string of expensive pearls that's disappeared. That three-member family has slimmed down to one member. And that single survivor stands to collect the whole bundle. All for herself."

He fitted the hat on his head and glared at me. "That's why. The Baron killed the old servant. Okay, I've bought that. But who killed him? And who killed his wife?" He squared around and stuck out his jaw. "I'm looking for the kid sister now. If you find out where she is. don't go mousing around with a straw skimmer and a five-pound box of cherry chocolates. What you do is call me. Any time of night or day. I can do without sleep when I have to. Just call me. Simple. Easy."

He turned and strode toward the door. I said, "I'm all impressed and shivery. And if you think I'm likely to follow that kind of orders, given in that tone of voice, you've got planters' warts where your brain ought to be."

He jerked the door open. "I overlooked the Avon Place bit for reasons we don't have to go in to. Right now I'm fresh out of consideration. Think it over, Steve. Don't even start to cross me."

The door slammed shut.

You big Mick cop, I almost yelled, but I choked it back and grabbed my drink. I finished all of it but the cubes. Then I flipped on the pre-amp and fitted a reel on the Ampex. Turning the volume up loud I watched the glassware dance on the tables. Finally I eased it off and sat down and tried to think.

After a while the telephone began to ring.

CHAPTER THIRTEEN

It was Megan, of course. Voice slightly frayed but buoyed with the resilience of youth. I said, "Where are you?"

"I'm at the Hotel Sydney. Do you know it?"

"What room?"

"Eight-fifteen. Are you going to—?"

"Seen the evening papers yet?"

"No. I don't usually... Why? What's happened?"

"I'm coming over."

"Well... Of course I want to see you, but—"

"Ten minutes," I said and hung up.

I strapped on my shoulder holster, picked up the pistol from the table and jammed it where it belonged. Then I pulled on a coat and went out.

The Sydney was on Vermont Avenue in a zone not yet totally commercial. A big, ungraceful graystone building with fire escapes zigzagging down the sides. Respectably middle-class, light on tourist trade, and catering to woman executives and ladies in comfortable retirement. As, I walked toward it, it impressed me as a secure refuge for a nineteen-year-old foreign girl.

The gray-haired man-hater at the desk gave me a steely stare as I strolled past and got into the self-service elevator. I could visualize her in bygone years dominating fifth grade math like a drill sergeant. A tweaker of noses and heavy on the dunce cap and ruler.

The elevator smelled vaguely of cooking. Of ancient hot-plate meals and hall disinfectant. The Sydney would stand four square for virtue and the Epworth League.

The hall runner had a dim flowered design where the pattern still showed. Eight-fifteen was halfway down the hall. A varnished door with pewter numerals. I knocked.

Running footsteps. The door swung open and I saw Megan. Behind her an open paper littered the bed. Her face was tight and drawn. "Couldn't you have told me?" she said bitterly.

"Bad news by phone sounds twice as bad." I closed the door.

"Could it be any worse?"

"Yes," I said. "Instead of your sister it could have been you."

She turned and walked toward the bed, dropped onto it and buried her face in her hands. Her shoulders began to shake. Sobs racked her throat. Comforting her would only prolong it. I lighted a cigarette and sat down in an armchair beside the bed.

After a while the sobbing ceased, she lowered her hands and stared at me with reddened eyes. "Why?" she whispered. "Why was my sister killed?"

"I don't know. I thought you might."

She shook her head dumbly, reached for a corner of the sheet and dried her eyes. Her fingers took my cigarette. Inhaling deeply, she straightened and stared up at the ceiling. Then she gave me back the cigarette. "I'm all right now," she said calmly. "It's just that I had no one to … that I'm so horribly alone now."

"Captain Kellaway came to my apartment to tell me about it. He was upset because he couldn't find you. The police like to know where people are. So do bonding companies."

"I'm sorry. I never thought to call. It looks as if I were hiding." She leaned over and reached for the telephone, but I pushed her arm aside.

"There's time for that," I said. "Let's think it over first."

Her brows furrowed.

I said, "Why would a man like Mario Garaldo know Wells and a tough named Ducky Macaluso?"

"Does he know Wells?"

"He does."

"The other name—I don't know it at all."

I jostled cigarette ash into a tray. "Garaldo must have come here to settle the score with Alejandro. Can we agree on that?"

"I . . . suppose so."

"He knew about the pearls? Knew Alejandro had bought them?"

She shrugged. "He might have. Why do you ask?"

"Because if he couldn't get at the numbered accounts in Switzerland he might have decided to settle for the pearls. Considering the fact that Garaldo had been cheated by Alejandro it's reasonable he might have gone to the house last night and demanded a settlement. Failing which he killed Alejandro and stole the pearls."

She bit her lip, her eyes widened and she said, "I don't think it happened that way."

"Neither do I." Stubbing out the cigarette, I leaned forward. "The two loaded pistols bother me. When was the second one loaded, and why? When Anita showed them to me only one was loaded. I know because I snapped the unloaded one. One thought occurs, though: that the second Manton pistol was loaded by someone who hoped Alejandro might harm himself with it, false-firing it or something like that. Loading a flintlock isn't easy unless you've seen it done. Then it's no trick to duplicate. Would you know how to load one?"

She seemed to shrink into the bed. "No," she breathed. "No. I don't know."

"Anita would have known. She handled them familiarly. She must have seen her husband load them."

"Yes. Anita knew how."

"Or Wells," I said slowly.

"Perhaps."

I shook out another cigarette and lighted it. "I can think of something else, Megan: someone who wanted to get close to Alejandro with a loaded pistol could have loaded the second one, waited until Alejandro took out the case, then taken the supposedly unloaded pistol and put it to his temple. To Alejandro it would have seemed an innocent gesture. Until the ball tore into his head."

Her body stiffened. "You think Anita did that?"

"I think it's possible. She hated Alejandro. Wells was her lover and Mario Garaldo was in town. She had a surplus of men. Maybe it was time to trim the number down."

"But you were with us when Anita came back. You saw how she—"

"A drunk act isn't hard to fake. She wasn't over at a Virginia drive-in with Wells, either. They were together in the Avon Place love nest. The place where Anita was killed this afternoon."

"How do you know that?"

"Because I saw her go there earlier last night. How long she stayed I don't know. Let's suppose Al got drunk and turned in. That gave her all the time in the world to run back to the house, kill Alejandro and get back to the apartment again. Ready to make an entrance later. As she did."

"A horrible thought."

"Why so horrible? You've told me how Alejandro used Anita. You've as much as told me he killed Lucia—and the police confirm that, by the way. What's so horrible about a murderer being killed, Megan? A man you hated."

Her face turned away from me. "One thinks about killing, even talks about it… but doing it is another thing."

I shook my head. "Dreams can merge with reality. He made a whore of your sister. If you married before his death you were cut out of his will. You feared him and Lucia Melho had something you thought would protect you. What was it, Megan?"

Her breasts were heaving. Her hands balled into tight little fists. Her face lifted and her lips parted. Hoarsely she said, "We were living together in Lisbon, the three of us. I was thirteen. Anita needed an operation. She was at the hospital three days. Three nights..." Her voice grew thin and bitter. "He came to my room. I didn't know why. It was dark. He lay on the bed beside me, told me he was lonely, worried over Anita. He kissed me. He'd kissed me before, but never like that. I didn't understand. I was only a child. I didn't know what he was doing, I begged him to go away but he only laughed and in the dark his face was the face of the devil. But he wouldn't go away. He kept kissing me, insisting. He was stronger than I was, much stronger. Finally he forced me. Afterward when he went away I thought of killing myself. I wish I had. Because that wasn't enough. He came back the next night. And the next."

The cords in her neck stood out like wires, her fingers were clawing the bed. "After Anita came home he'd come to my bed early in the morning. Nobody knew. Not even Anita then. Only Lucia. Lucia knew because she found us together. She found us together many times...." Her voice trailed away. Her eyes closed while the knives of memory cut her apart.

My guts were frozen. I wanted to say something, stop her. I had heard enough. Far too much. I opened my mouth but nothing came out.

"Lucia went to a priest and swore to what she had seen in my bedroom. The priest signed the paper. Then Lucia put it away. When Alejandro came again I told him what Lucia had done. I made him let me go away to school." Her eyes opened slowly. They were dull eyes. Her breathing slowed and her hands uncurled. Her head dropped and she whispered, "That is my life. That is my shame."

I wet my lips. When words came my voice was hoarse, off-key. "How could you blame yourself?"

"I should have killed him then. I blame myself because I did not. I did not and someone else did. Someone with less reason."

I moved over and took her hands. “I’m glad you didn’t.”

She nodded slowly, put one hand to her forehead distractedly. “What right did I have to call my sister a whore? What else was I?”

I pressed her fingers against my lips. Then I kissed them. They were like frozen flesh. Finally they warmed. After a while she drew away. “How can you do that when you know about me? How can you—”

“He’s dead,” I snapped. “That changes everything. That’s how you’ve got to think of it. You sent me to get the paper from Lucia but by then he’d killed her and destroyed the affidavit. There’s nothing left. Let the memory die too.”

Her hand lifted and her fingers touched my hair. “Thank you,” she said quietly. “Oh, thank you for that. I’ve never known anyone like you before. Never anyone so kind.”

My throat tightened. I took a deep breath and said, “I was in the apartment when Anita was killed today. The killer wanted it to look as if I had done it.”

She shrank away from me. “Do the police think you killed her?”

I shook my head. “Kellaway knows how it happened, but not who did it. Or for what reason. I think I do.”

“Why?”

“For the pearls. The killer must have thought she took them after Alejandro was dead. I don’t think he got them from Anita because I don’t think she had them. But I don’t think he’ll stop there. Wherever they are, he’ll try to get them. You’re safe here, Megan, even the police don’t know where you are. For now I don’t want even them to know. Tonight and tomorrow I want you to stay here. Don’t go out. Don’t open the door for anyone but me. Do you understand?”

She nodded silently and I stood up. “You were upstairs when Alejandro was killed. You must have heard the shot.”

“I did,” she said evenly.

"What did you do then?"

Her eyebrows lifted. "I did nothing."

"Why?"

Her voice hardened. "I hoped he might be dead. At first I thought he might have killed himself. Then I thought Anita—I mean someone—might have shot him. In either case I was satisfied. He deserved his death."

"How long after the shot did you call me?"

"At least a half an hour." She stood up. "I lay in my bed praying that he was dead. I remembered all those nights, all those mornings with him, his cruelty, his bestiality, and I prayed that I was free of him at last. When I went down and found him dead it was the answer to my prayers."

I nodded. I could imagine her up in the canopied bed, eyes closed, tense, remembering the way her sister's husband had debauched her, then walking quietly down through the silent house to the library where her seducer lay dead. It would have taken steel nerve for that, but the motive was there. Ample motive.

I said, "Is Wells still at the house?"

She nodded. "I told him to be gone by tomorrow."

"Where's his room?"

"Above the garage. Steve, please don't do anything that might—"

"Hurt me?" I finished.

"Yes."

I kissed her cheek gently. "That's the least of our worries. I'll have Molly come and stay with you."

"No. I'll do as you said. I'll stay here. I'll be all right."

"Sure?"

She gave me a brave smile. I turned and walked to the door, went out and listened until she had chained the door inside. Then I straightened my shoulders and went down the hall to the elevator.

Everything normal in the lobby. All the silent trappings of genteel decay. I went out of the door, crossed the street and got into my car.

At first I didn't see him in the darkness, I only felt his presence. Then I turned and saw the gun. He held it lightly on his thigh, the muzzle pointing at me. It was an automatic pistol. My gaze traveled up until it rested on his face.

He was a dapper-looking fellow in a fly-front town coat, a silver-gray tie and white starched collar. The rim of his Homburg shadowed his plump oval face, but it was a face I had seen before. The lips opened and the voice said coldly, "Do not be difficult, Meestair Bentley. I am quite ready to keel you."

I sucked air into my lungs. "I thought you'd gotten tired of our little town and shoved off. But of course you couldn't leave without the pearls."

CHAPTER FOURTEEN

Garaldo's eyes glinted like agates. "We will talk of those pearls, Meestair Bentley. Now drive to Esquivel's house."

"There's nobody there," I said. "Only ghosts."

The little gun jabbed into my ribs. I shoved the key into the ignition, started the engine and pulled out into traffic.

By looking sideways I could see his face, lighted briefly by street lights. It was the face of a man in his late forties, plump but not soft. The lips were hard, the eyes old. The face of a man who had learned how to survive.

Logan Circle. The Martin Luther statue. Then Massachusetts to Q. North and onto R Street. A dark night. No moon. I had lost track of time.

"The pearls," Garaldo's voice said distantly. "Esquivel cheated me of a fortune. All that is left are the pearls."

"You can't sell them. They're known."

That got a sardonic laugh. "In Europe anything can be sold. Or in Cairo or Istanbul. The thought is insignificant."

Past Montrose Park. Past Dumbarton Oaks, and finally the hulking outline of a dark witches' roost. I slowed the car and said, "What makes you think I know anything about the pearls?"

He leaned toward me. "The night Esquivel died you were here even before the police. And you made love to Anita."

"That was hardly a distinction."

His hand flicked out and slapped hard across my mouth. My head snapped back and my tongue tasted salt and iron. Wet and warm.

"She was my woman," he rasped. "I think you keeled her. To get the pearls."

I wiped blood from my lips on the back of my hand. "She was anybody's woman. For anyone with the time and the inclination, and you know it. Try another chivalrous slap and I'll sink my thumbs in your throat. The place where she was killed was her own little hideaway. She didn't keep it for me, Garaldo."

His eyes were slits in a rubber mask. "You lie, Bentley."

I shrugged. "Ask Wells who had an extra key."

He grunted and gestured with the pistol. I turned the wheels up through the open gate. When I began to brake, he motioned me ahead. I drove on back to the concrete turnaround. The headlights played on the doors of the big garage. Garaldo reached forward and snicked them off. He opened his door and got out. So far he hadn't frisked me. The Walther was still under my left arm. It was a detail he had overlooked. In America young gentlemen don't go heeled. But then I wasn't a young gentleman.

Opening the door I got out on the concrete. The night air seemed to be laced with tendrils of fog. I turned and glanced up at the house. No lights. Not even a candle glow in Molly's garret. Nothing. I was alone and covered by a gun. I shivered.

Somewhere a door opened. The sound came from around the side of the garage, a grating wooden sound like a coffin lowering.

Out of the darkness came a man. On the concrete his rubber-soled shoes made hardly a sound. They whispered like wind at a mortuary window. The man beckoned. "This way, Mr. Garaldo."

Al Wells. Welinsky. I wondered what part he was to play. Garaldo made a motion with his head and I began walking toward the chauffeur. Garaldo fell in behind.

Al turned and disappeared around the corner of the garage. I followed and stepped through a door. Wooden steps led to a loft above the garage. They creaked under our weight. At the top of the steps another door.

A room. Not large, not small. Gloomy, furnished with hand-me-down furniture, a scarred radio and an old TV. Curtains across the window. A telephone. A day bed and two closed doors.

Al turned to me. His eyes were circled, his face hollow. He needed a shave. His eyes surveyed the room and his mouth twisted. “It ain’t much, is it, Bentley?”

“For you, just about right.”

He danced over toward me, feinted with his left and sank his right in my guts. I doubled over, clutching at the pain and Garaldo shouted something. Al backed away, his face murderous.

A thin red cloud blanketed my eyes. Air whistled through my throat. I straightened slowly. “I’ll remember that, you bastard,” I snarled.

“Do that little thing,” he jeered. “Only you ain’t got long to remember. Unless you come up with the pearls you took from the Baron.”

Garaldo came into my line of vision. His jaw was set. The pistol muzzle bobbed at me. “The pearls,” he snapped. “Where are they?”

“Ask Al.”

Garaldo’s eyebrows lifted. “Why Al?”

“You hired him to get them, didn’t you? Him and Macaluso.”

“I never touched them,” Al growled. “Hell, I never got the chance. The Baron was dead and the safe was locked. What the hell could I do?”

“You might have thought of that,” Garaldo said, “before you keeled him.”

Al glanced at me uneasily. “I didn’t kill him. I told you that.”

I laughed at him.

He began to move toward me but Garaldo’s gun motioned him back. Al said, “Listen, Mr. Garaldo, I played it straight with you.”

“You play something straight?” I said. “You’d sell out your mother for a zinc dollar.”

Al's face looked like a block of cement. "You son of a bitch, I'll kill you."

"I'm not particular who does the job. But to clear the air, you might tell Mr. Garaldo who had the other key to Anita's nest on Avon Place."

Fear Hashed across his face like a darting bat. He licked his lips. Garaldo turned and stared at him.

I said, "The night the Baron was killed they were together, Garaldo. Your woman and Al here. How long, I don't know. But I saw her go into the place and there was someone waiting. Someone who'd entered before her. Someone with a key."

Garaldo sat down suddenly, heavily. Now the pistol was pointing at both of us. The scene was improving. It was playing better. Much better. But there was room for improvement. Plenty of room.

"What was Anita to you, you cheap hoodlum?" Garaldo grated.

"Nothing, Mr. Garaldo. I swear we never—"

I laughed again. A long jeering laugh that cut him off. Al's fists clenched. He turned to me, his face furious. "God damn you, you laid her yourself."

"Never slander the dead, Al. Besides, we're talking about you—the guy with a key to the love nest. The man who strangled Anita had a key, too."

"Basta!" Garaldo barked and looked at me. "What do you know of her death?"

I reached for a cigarette, pulled out the pack slowly and selected one. Then I lighted it, praying no one noticed the way my fingers shook. I leaned on the edge of the table and looked down at Garaldo. His eyes were heavy. The eyes of a man who cared little whether he lived or died.

I said, "Anita called me this afternoon. She said she wanted me to come to her. She didn't say why. Her voice was paralyzed by terror. I got over there as soon as I could. The door opened and I saw her. She screamed and a pipe hit the back of my head. When I came to she was dead. I went away and called the police."

"He's lying!" Al shouted. "He killed her himself!"

"Tell me why I killed her."

"For the pearls."

I gave what I hoped was a sarcastic laugh. "Stick to the same story, Al. A minute ago I'd taken the pearls the night before—after the Baron was dead. Which way was it?"

Al wiped his mouth with the back of his hand.

Garaldo's eyes widened with interest.

I said, "If I got the pearls the night before I had no reason to kill Anita today. Or looking at it another way, I didn't kill her and I never had the pearls. But someone has them. And someone killed Anita." I was staring at Al. "The air stinks with double-cross. Take his key ring, Garaldo. Try them over at Avon Place. Let's see who's lying—who double-crossed who."

Garaldo was staring at Al. "Well," he said slowly, "the keys."

Al's eyes darted from Garaldo to me and back again. A muscle was working in his face. There was sweat on his upper lip. "Lissen, Mr. Garaldo," he whispered, "she gave me the key. I couldn't help it. Nobody could."

Garaldo's lips looked like an ax slash in oak. "Very well," he said softly. "You betrayed me. You made love to my woman and you lied to me. Did you keel her as well?"

"Jesus, no, Mr. Garaldo. Why would I do a thing like that?" He was shaking all over. He was a man staring at the face of death.

"Why did you lie to me?" Garaldo got up slowly. In his hand the gun was as big as a cannon.

I said, "He lied because his kind always does. You hired him to steal something of yours from Esquivel, but he couldn't stick to that. He wasn't smart enough to get the pearls on his own. Laying Anita was easier. That's what you got for your money, Garaldo."

Garaldo was still staring at Al. "Answer me. Did you keel her?"

Al's jaw hung open. It closed feebly a couple of times but no sound came out.

I was liking the scene better all the time. I was loving it. Garaldo seemed to have forgotten me. I could have whipped out the Walther and shot them both but there was more to be said. Quite a bit more. In the room there was less sound than a graveyard.

I broke the silence. "Let's go back a ways, Garaldo. Back to when the Baron was killed. Back to someone doctoring the other Manton pistol, loading it so that both were loaded. The Baron knew you were in town. He was afraid of you. Enough afraid to ask for police protection. Who told him you were here?"

"I did," Garaldo said. "I called the swine and threatened him."

I nodded. "That set the wheels in motion. The night before, the Baron had killed old Lucia Melho to rid himself of the threat of blackmail. The police know that and they've written off the case. To the two women in this house, and possibly to others, the death of Lucia was the handwriting on the wall. It meant Esquivel had gotten desperate. So someone loaded the other Manton pistol. Someone who had figured out a clever way to get rid of the Baron. Someone who wanted him dead. Someone who figured his death could be made to pass as suicide. His plea to the police may have suggested that. Now, who loaded the pistol? Anita could have done it. So could Al here. Even you."

"Yes," Garaldo said. "Even I."

I inhaled and let smoke drift across the room. The air was still. We were in a sealed capsule a thousand feet under the sea. Dead men talking without hope.

"The pistol was loaded, turning a harmless museum-piece into a deadly weapon, unknown to the Baron. Yesterday evening Al goes down to Avon Place and lets himself into the apartment. Later Anita runs down to join him. Still later a shot is fired in the Baron's study and the Baron's body is discovered by Megan. She calls me and I arrive and get in touch with the police. Then Anita returns—apparently drunk."

Something flickered in Garaldo's eyes. To Al he said, "You spent a pleasant evening with my woman? Were her lips warm and inviting? Her body supple and sweet?"

Al's hands opened and closed helplessly. "We... we had a few drinks, Mr. Garaldo. After a while she said she had to go back to—"

"Lies!" Garaldo spat, and the pistol barrel jerked upward.

I plucked the cigarette from my dry lips. "I think one of them came back to the house, got the Baron to take out the pistols, picked up the one that was supposedly unloaded and shot him from close range. Then laid the pistol down where it would look like suicide and left the house quickly. Possibly by the study window. Or even by the front door."

"Who did it?" Garaldo snarled. "You or Anita? Who took the pearls? Tell me or I will keel you!"

Al's fingers clawed his throat. "She did it," he whispered. "We worked out an alibi together. Only she got drunk afterward. I could hardly get her out the door."

"She took the pearls?" Garaldo rasped.

"No, She... she said she didn't. Jesus, maybe she did."

I said, "Someone thought she had the pearls. That's why she was killed."

Garaldo lifted the pistol. He lined it carefully to point at Al's belly. "So you keeled her," he said in a voice like death itself. "Tell me why I should not keel you now?"

I pushed away from the table. Slowly. I didn't want to excite Garaldo, push him over the edge. "He's still lying," I said. "I think Anita loaded the pistol and Al killed the Baron. Only he doesn't have guts enough to admit it. Look at him shake, Garaldo. He's half dead already. You won't get the truth from him."

Garaldo's face turned slightly toward me. "Then he took the pearls?"

"He could have," I said. "I think he killed the Baron because it was something Anita suggested. He's enough of a lout to fall for the let's-get-rid-of-hubby pitch. Especially when delivered as convincingly as Anita could. I think he wanted her for himself and the pearls were secondary. And there was the problem of the locked safe."

Garaldo was gazing at Al again. "How did you solve that?" he asked gutturally.

Al moved his head weakly. He was on the verge of blubbering.

I said, "A dial combination isn't an easy thing to change. Let's assume the safe was open when Esquivel took the house. The Falconer sisters were dead—theoretically no one else knew the combination. Let's assume he never changed the combination at all. Now, old ladies get forgetful as the years go on and I wouldn't be surprised if they'd written the combination elsewhere—in the family Bible, or in a list of telephone numbers, or even on a scrap of paper shoved in the back of a drawer. Someone in the house could have found it. Someone who wanted what the safe contained: the pearls." I sucked in heavy air and went on. "Several people could have made that discovery: Anita, Megan, Molly or Al. Take your choice. We're agreed that Al killed the Baron. If he had the safe combination, too, that was his chance to take the pearls and get out. That way he had the woman *and* the pearls."

Garaldo's mouth made a sound as though he were tasting something as bitter as alum. He took a step toward Al. A short step heavy with menace. Al began to back away. Black stubble stood away from the white flesh of his face as though he were already dead. He croaked, "She musta took the pearls herself, Mr. Garaldo. I swear to God I never seen them."

"The time is too late for prayers," Garaldo said thickly. "Give me the pearls or I keel you now."

Al's teeth were chattering. "I never…" he began, and then his mouth clicked shut as though another idea had come to him.

"She took the pearls. Sure, that's how it was. She took them herself and Macaluso killed her to get them."

Garaldo's eyes were slits. "Macaluso?" he said softly.

Al's head nodded frantically, jerkily, like a starving chicken. "Sure, Macaluso done it. He killed her. He's got the pearls." The words came in a rush, like marbles tumbling from a broken bag.

My stomach was as hard as grapeshot. I undid my coat button carefully and straightened my shoulders.

"Macaluso," Garaldo sneered. "Anything to save your rotten life."

The sound came slowly, eerily, a scrape like a broken branch. A screech of wood on wood. A door was opening.

One of the closed doors. It opened just wide enough to let a pistol poke through. I stared at the blued barrel of an automatic five yards away and I began to move back. Garaldo couldn't see it but Al could. *"Ducky!"* he screamed. *"Don't—"*

The bark of the pistol cut him off. Two shots so fast they echoed as one. Al grabbed at his stomach and his knees bent. He went down slowly, a hideous grin Stretching his face. Then the wire snapped and he crumpled forward. The door slammed aside and Ducky Macaluso stepped out. "The son of a bitch," he snarled, "trying to finger me for what he done!"

His face turned slowly toward Garaldo. "I'll take care of this," he said. "Only you an' me'll ever know." His gun arm dropped beside his thigh. The rank stench of guncotton filled the air.

I coughed. I wanted to retch.

Macaluso's eyes reached past Garaldo and settled on me as if he were seeing me for the first time. A crooked grin spread over his face. "Hello, sucker," he said. "Long time no see."

"Not so long," I said. "Only as long ago as this afternoon. When you sapped me and killed Garaldo's woman."

CHAPTER FIFTEEN

Macaluso uttered a short ugly laugh. "You got a slim chance to get out of this alive, fella. Al spoke outa turn. Keep it up and you'll get the same."

Macaluso turned back to Garaldo. "Al killed the dame," he said. "Al was nuts about her but you was in town and so she gave him the old heaveroo. He couldn't take it. So he put the black belt around her throat and pulled it tight. That way she didn't go with nobody."

"What color belt?" I said.

"Black—it was..." His eyes darted from Garaldo to me and back again. "Hell, the color don't make no difference." He licked his lips uncertainly.

I laughed shortly. "I think only the man who strangled her would know what color the belt was. What do you think, Mr. Garaldo?"

Macaluso's gun arm lifted, the muzzle covered me. "Big mouth, you'll get it now."

A shot exploded. I dropped to the floor and whipped out my Walther. Another shot. I had him at the end of my sights but already he was falling, his face frozen in total surprise. He was dead before he hit the floor. I rolled over and looked up at Garaldo. A wisp of smoke curled out of the muzzle of his gun. He stared at it and suddenly he sat down. I pulled myself up and stuck the Walther back where it belonged.

"Thanks," I said and heard my voice crack. "He was your last chance to get the pearls."

Garaldo nodded slowly. His hand seemed welded to the gun. My ears were still ringing from the shooting. The bodies lay within two yards of each other. Sacks of old clothes now. Garaldo's shot had caught Macaluso just under the chin. Macaluso's shot had been reflex action, fired after he was dead. I turned and glanced around at the ceiling. High on the wall was a small hole in the painted plasterboard.

Garaldo stared at me. "You knew," he said dully. "You could have told me."

"You weren't in a mood to listen," I said. "You were pumped full of wrong leads by Al and Ducky. I had to find a chink somewhere. You see it now because of the way things worked out. And I never argue with a man who's got a gun in my ribs."

He glanced down at the gun again as though he wanted to free himself of it. I went over to him and detached it from his fingers. Then I got out a handkerchief and polished it carefully.

Garaldo looked up at me. "The police will not like that."

"They'll love it," I said, went over to Al's body and bent down. I clasped the dead fingers around the automatic and then I let it drop. At the thud Garaldo started. Then he covered his face with his hands.

My cigarette was burning through the rug. I stamped it out and said, "We're wasting time."

He pulled himself out of the chair, blinked and shook himself. Then he straightened his tie. His glance fastened on the telephone.

"Not yet," I said.

He turned and came toward me. "You had a gun," he said. "You could have shot me."

"I'm careful who I shoot," I said. "I'm just as glad it was you who shot Macaluso."

"I, too. For Anita." Turning he spat on Macaluso's body.

Covering my hand with the handkerchief I opened the stair door and waited until he was past me. Then I pulled it shut and followed him down. As we walked toward the car I saw a flash of white in the shadows near the house. Moving toward it, I pulled out the Walther and said, "Come out."

A figure moved out of the shadows. Someone small. Her shoes made little rasping noises on the concrete.

"Closer," I said, "the light's none too good."

She came toward me and I saw Molly. There was a shawl around her shoulders and her white maid's collar stood out starkly.

She said, "I heard shooting."

I dropped the pistol back into its holster. "That you did. But not by this gun."

She shivered.

I said, "Call the police, Molly. Tell them what you heard but don't mention me. My car was never here. I was never here. Nor my friend."

She glanced past me at Garaldo getting into the Olds.

"For Miss Megan," I said.

She nodded slowly, bent toward me and whispered something in my ear. I felt my jaw muscles set. Then she moved back into the shadows. I got into the Olds, started the engine and turned onto the drive. I kept the lights off until I was two blocks from the house. Then I put them on, reached into the glove compartment and handed the bottle to Garaldo.

He shook his head.

While he held the wheel I polished the rim and tilted the bottle. The liquor trickled down like frozen blood.

I had felt weak but strength was flowing back. I tilted the bottle again and then I capped it and put it away. Garaldo said, "You are a curious man. I thought in this country things were done only for money. But in all of this there is no money for you."

"None at all." We were driving down Wisconsin. The neon lights looked friendly. I was grateful for the sight of sidewalk strollers, the young, the old, the lovers and the lonely.

Garaldo said, "Is that all you have to say?"

I pulled out a crumpled pack of cigarettes and lighted one. "I found a girl one day," I said. "Thrown from her horse. She was frightened, she needed help."

"Only that?"

"Only that," I said as we turned onto M Street. "Who wrote you telling you where the Baron could be found? Anita?"

"Yes. She said she could get the pearls and we would go away together. She said we could trust Wells and Wells found Macaluso. I paid them both—to protect Anita and to help her get the pearls. Now—" He shrugged and looked away.

There was a cab stand and waiting cabbies. The glow of their cigarettes looked like fireflies in the night. I pulled into line and braked the Olds behind the last cab. Garaldo looked at me questioningly.

I said, "You have a plane ticket. Use it."

He nodded stiffly. Then he got out and walked up to the first taxi. I backed away and pulled out into the street again. As I passed his cab I could see him sitting back against the cushion, his eyes closed as though he were asleep. For a foreigner, unused to our ways, it must have been a trying day.

His pearls were gone but he would survive. He would go back to Europe now, become part of the shadowy background of foreign finance and manipulation and then he would emerge again. In a year or two he would have a fortune once more, an estate in Burgos and a summer home along the Basque coast, a yacht and a house in Paris. He could get along without the golden pearls.

I drove on M as far as the first all-night drugstore, went in and rang Artie's home. When he answered his voice was excited. "Where the hell you been, Steve?"

"Out and around."

"Well, so's Ducky Macaluso. He came back to the Hotel Bedford and the boys trailed him from there. I guess he was looking for Garaldo."

"Probably. Where'd he go?"

"Hold tight—he went into the Avon Place apartment."

"No kidding."

"The boys got a description of the dame who rents apartment Number two. It fits the Baroness."

"Whaddaya know," I murmured. "By any chance do you subscribe to the evening papers?"

"I read the sports page every night."

"Fine," I said. "Pick me a winner, will you? Fourth at Belmont tomorrow."

I hung up. Macaluso had gone to the apartment after Anita was there. I liked it a little better that way. I hadn't liked thinking she had wanted me put away. I thought about calling Megan but she would be asleep by now. Tomorrow would be time enough.

Tomorrow Kellaway would have news for me. He would enjoy telling me about it. A wrap-up. Everything in a tidy package. Even to Artie's boys having seen Macaluso go into Anita's apartment. Three cases solved for the price of one. Or was it five?

The liquor was fuming through my brain. I was glassy-eyed. I felt as if a tractor had dragged me over half of Maryland. I pushed the booth door aside and blinked at the staring lights. My hand still trembled. There was an answer for that. I got back in my car and drove slowly out to my apartment.

As I dropped into bed I thought of the room over the garage, floodlighted and busy with police photographers and fingerprint experts: dactylographers they called them now. Everything in police work was scientific these days. Crime labs and test tubes and chemists in white coats, and still murderers got away. I could see the clean-up boys carrying two sheeted bodies down the steep stairway, cursing at the weight and wrestling the heavy baskets out of the doorway to the waiting meat wagon. Police work. The hell with it.

Turning out the lights, I thought again about calling Megan, but she deserved a good night's sleep. I remembered what had happened to her when she was thirteen. It would take a lot to make up for that. All the Baron's money and then some. If any of it could be found.

I thought about it for a long time and then I got up and took a Nembutal to calm down. For one day I had seen a lot of death. I would see it again in nightmares for years to come. The black belt. A slip of the tongue and death takes over.

After a while I drifted away into nothingness.

I was fixing coffee when Kellaway came by. He was in an expansive mood. My mouth tasted like the bottom of a GI can. I told him so.

He chuckled patronizingly. "While you were tying on the bonnet last night things were happening. Seen the papers yet?"

"My eyes are still taped shut."

"This younger generation," he said. "No get-up-and-go any more. A generation of sack-lovers. Where's the old frontier spirit gone to?"

"They gave it back to the Indians." I filled our cups and sat down. "You're oozing more good will than a TV comedian. Break the suspense."

He gave me a glance of measured distaste. "It happens there were two men Al Welinsky and Ducky Macaluso. You remember them, don't you?"

"I may," I said. "The world moves so fast a fellow can barely keep track anymore."

He jerked his cigar out of his mouth. "If I thought this was a set-up you'll engineered, I'd—"

"You'll do what?" I said. "If you were smart, you'd let slip a word of appreciation now and then. But never that for the nameless helpers who labor unseen. The narrow view is that unless it's done by a bull in blue serge and brass buttons it doesn't count. I associate you with that view. Tell me I'm wrong."

He rolled the cigar between his thumb and forefinger. "Hell," he said finally. "Read it in the papers."

"Come on," I urged. "Moments ago you were the big chesty cop grandly patronizing the civilian outsider. Let's have it. With diagrams. Play it big."

His eyes were wounded. "You held out on me, you bastard."

I shrugged. "Think back to the terms we parted on last night. There was some table-slamming and several dire warnings on your part if I remember accurately. Is that any way to inspire confidence?"

He lifted his cup and drained it. "All right," he said bitterly. "Who killed who?"

I sipped coffee, put down the cup and said, "Al killed the Baron and Macaluso killed Anita. Then they killed each other."

"Why?"

The muffins popped out of the toaster and I buttered them and added a little English marmalade. When I was munching comfortably I said, "Al had a yen for Anita and figured the Baron as the only obstacle. Anita wanted the pearls and the Baron was the obstacle there. Between Al and Anita the Baron got the long leap."

"Who got the pearls?"

"Anita could have gotten them," I said. "It's hard for a husband to keep household secrets from a wife, and she could have come across the safe combination in a diligent search carried out over a period of time. As soon as the Baron was dead she could have opened the safe and carried away the pearls. At least one person figured she had: Macaluso. That's why he killed her. I think he just put the belt around her neck to scare her, make her come through with the pearls, but he didn't realize how easy it is to choke someone."

"That answers one question anyway," Kellaway said, and rubbed the side of his face, leaving a reddened mark. "Why Macaluso killed her. Dead she couldn't tell anything at all. Now what about Al and Macaluso?"

"That's for the kindergarten class. Thieves quarreling over the spoils."

He stuck the cigar in his mouth, puffed it and stared up at the ceiling. I started on my second muffin. Mighty tasty.

After a while Kellaway said, "The report will show it that way, but if they were arguing over the pearls, where were they? Where are they now?"

"Did you check Al's room?"

"We tore it apart."

"The Avon Place apartment?"

"Likewise," he said sourly.

"They could be anywhere. If Macaluso got them from Anita he had a world of time to hide them away. A safe deposit box, for example."

"That would be sweet," Kellaway said heavily. "He might as well have dropped them into the Bay."

I nodded and lighted a cigarette, flipped the match at the sink and missed. My distance judgment was going to the poodles.

I said, "Anita had time to stick them away in one of the dusty crannies in that old monstrosity. Maybe the mice have chewed them up for calcium by now."

He gazed at me disgustedly. "You get less helpful as the morning wears on."

"Anyway," I said, "the pearls belong to the surviving heir. Or heiress, in this case. They're insured. Seventy thousand dollars' worth. She doesn't stand to lose if they don't turn up."

"That ain't the point, Steve. The insurance company's offering a twenty per cent reward if we find them. That would make fourteen thousand dollars for the Police Benevolent Fund."

"Well," I said. "Lots of luck. More coffee?"

He shook his head and stood up. "I should be in your kind of business," he said. "Rooms full of lovely dames and no reports to write."

"You wouldn't like it," I said. "The body takes too much punishment. Not to mention the morale."

"You're pretty cheerful for a fellow who was sapped yesterday p.m."

"I eat saps like macaroni," I told him. "But that doesn't make me smart."

"I wonder what does," he said and went out of the door.

I heard him plodding through the living room. Then the hall door opened and closed. Not too gently.

After a while I got up, piled the dishes in the sink, took a shower and shaved. I was tying my cravat when the telephone rang. Megan Dos Santos.

"Steve," she said, "you know about Wells and that other person, don't you?"

"Kellaway came by to tell me."

"It's in the papers this morning." There was a pause. Finally: "I wondered if you had anything to do with it?"

"Why don't we have lunch together and talk it over?"

"I was hoping you'd ask me. Let's do exactly what we did yesterday. And it's lovely enough for a sail."

I peered through the venetian blinds at the sun glinting on the leaves outside. "So it is. I hoped I might be able to interest you in boarding the boat again, and sure enough, you suggested it yourself."

"What time shall I meet you, Steve?"

"One o'clock," I said. "I'll be punctual."

"So will I." She hung up, but not until after I thought I had heard a kiss being breathed along the wires. Progress.

I drove downtown, parked and went up to the office.

Mrs. Bross said, "It's after eleven, Mr. Bentley. I was afraid you might be ill."

"So was I," I said, "but everything turned out for the best."

She gave me an odd look, dropped a stack of working papers on my desk and said, "You've been here so little lately I haven't known whether you'd be keeping any appointments I might make for clients."

"Give me just today," I said. "Monday, we'll put in a full day. Scout's honor." I made the three-fingered sign. She sniffed and went away.

I worked through the noon hour and then I got the Olds and drove to Maine Avenue.

It was spring's hottest day so far. I left my hat in the car, went into the club and climbed up to the observation deck.

She was waiting for me in a dress of sapphire blue, white gloves and white pumps. Around her neck hung the little gold chain and the twelfth century crucifix. She leaned forward and caught both my hands.

CHAPTER SIXTEEN

"Hello, Annie," I said cheerfully.

Her eyes questioned me.

"Little Orphan Annie," I said. "No mama, no papa, no Spearmint gum. No one but Daddy Warbucks and where the hell he is nobody ever knows." I sat down beside her and put my feet on a hassock. "A real character. But square."

In a troubled voice Megan said, "I don't think I understand what you mean."

I patted her hands. "Ignore it. We'll share a gourd of bubbly and some serious talk."

"About what, Steve?"

"Oh, life and things. You've got a whole big future ahead of you—yours to decide."

"I know," she said in a low voice. "I thought you might help me plan it."

"I'm old enough to have a few convictions," I said. "At least on the negative side. So I can tell you what *not* to do."

A waiter hovered over us. "Champagne cocktails," I told him. "Light on the foliage."

"Yes, suh." He went bobbing away, aluminum tray balanced as securely as on the nose of a circus seal.

She took out a cigarette, waited for me to light it and said, "You're in a curious mood today."

"Lack of sleep. I was up late last night. Jousting with death, you might say."

Her face tilted. "You *were* there, then. In Wells's room."

"I was indeed."

"Why did you go?"

"It was hardly my idea. When I left you last night there was someone waiting for me in my car. A man. He had a gun. His name was Mario Garaldo. He pointed the gun at me and told me where to drive. Your house was where he told me to go."

"Mario," she breathed. "What did he want, Steve?"

I saw the drinks coming from the bar. I lifted my feet from the hassock and sat up. "He had some sort of an idea I might have killed Anita. Or that I had the pearls." I turned and looked at her. "He kept talking about *his* pearls. Silly man."

Her eyebrows furrowed. I handed her one of the champagne glasses and lifted mine. "Here's to truth and clarity," I said. "And an end to confusion."

We drank together. The champagne was as cold as a glacial stream. It set my teeth on edge. I drank again and this time it was better.

Megan said, "What happened to Mario?"

"He couldn't find the pearls, so there was no point in staying around." I looked at her through the golden bubbles. "Before he went away last night he killed a man."

"He did?"

"Ducky Macaluso. One way of getting rid of unsatisfactory employees. But by then Macaluso had killed Al, so he probably had it coming to him. Mario had hired them both, you know, but they double-crossed him and each other. And Anita double-crossed the Baron and Al. Then yesterday Macaluso strangled Anita because he thought she had the pearls."

She stared at me, put the cigarette between her lips and kept on staring.

I said, "The whole thing adds up to a bumper crop of confusion. And Anita's death was a mistake." I sipped the cold champagne. Something was wrong with it. The taste was bitter. Spoiled.

She said calmly, “Death is unnecessary.”

“From a philosophical point of view. But sometimes death clears the air, cleanses falsehood, evens scores. As in the case of the Baron. Who mourns him, Megan?”

“No one,” she said quietly.

I said, “No one should be as beautiful as you. With you in the room nobody has a chance.”

She smiled prettily. “No one ever said that before.”

“You’ll hear it again,” I said. “You’ll hear it until you’ll be able to predict it in advance. You’ll know the tone, the nuance and the look in their eyes. You’ll get bored by it. You’ll become cynical over it.”

She shook her head slowly. “Never when it comes from you.”

“Very neat,” I said, put down my glass and picked up the menu. “I’m not up to seafood today. My stomach’s still asleep and I’ll have to wake it up gently. For you the same as yesterday?”

She nodded, picked up her glass and drained it. I called over a waiter and gave our order. A mutton chop for me with whipped potatoes. To ballast the moths in my stomach. The waiter brought more champagne and while we were killing it I told her what had happened last night. She said, “Then the police will not need me anymore?”

“There’s no reason they should. They didn’t find the pearls but they cleared up five killings. That’s a big day even in Washington.”

She smiled slightly. Her eyes held an elusive distant look. As though she were already surveying the high walls of old Castile.

The waiter came over, coughed, and I stood up and drew her to her feet. There was a canopy on the observation deck, shielding it from the sun. Our table was near the railing where we could look out over the channel to my boat nodding at its moorings like a drowsy water bird.

When she was seated she said, “Is it a fast boat, Steve?”

“We’ll race the gulls. You’ll see.”

She smiled at me again, reached over and clasped my hand. "Do many women fall in love with you?"

"Some weeks hardly any at all."

"Seriously."

I shrugged. "Love is a curious thing. A thing of the moment. It can visit you as briefly as a hummingbird or it can stay curled up as contentedly as a cat. And for a lifetime. That's a serious answer."

Her hand left mine and picked up her fork. Her face wore an uneasy expression. Perhaps before we parted she would tell me what was troubling her.

Lunch over we walked down to the boat landing and I helped her into the dory, grappled the oars and pulled us out to my boat. When she was standing beside the mainmast, I said, "You didn't bring your sailor suit, Megan. There's liable to be some water taken over the gunwales."

"I shouldn't have said I'd sail today. There isn't time enough. I have an appointment with Mr. Gurney at three—and other things to do." She smiled at me winningly. "Another day, Steve?"

"Sure. It's a bad day for me too." I moved back to the tiller, bent over and inspected the fittings. A fish swam close to the rudder. I jiggled the tiller and it darted away. I heard Megan go below, move forward toward the head.

After a while she came back, purse in one hand. I stood up and said, "If you're going to make that three o'clock date with Hod we'd better go back."

She came to me and laid one hand on my wrist. "I'm sorry, Steve. It was thoughtless of me."

I shook my head. "On the contrary. It was beautifully planned. All of it."

Her mouth opened and closed. The troubled look came back to her face. "What do you mean?"

"It was all planned," I said. "The only part I'm willing to believe was accidental was the fall from the horse. Otherwise the whole sequence was planned."

"Steve! Are you out of your mind?"

I shook my head. "Not any more. I think you've suspected I knew but you came here anyway. Because you had to come."

My fingers tightened around her hand. The one that held the purse. She tried to twist free. Her face was agonized. She said, *"Let go!"*

I laughed. "That's a silly little purse. It only cost you five dollars. I'll buy it from you for twenty."

Her face hardened. "What would you do with it?"

"Throw it overboard."

Her eyes flared wide. "Take me back to shore."

"In time," I said and pried the purse from her fingers. She snatched at it, clawing to get it back but I turned away. "Careful," I warned. "It's a small boat. I'd hate to fish you out dripping wet. You'd be late at the lawyer's office, and the law is very important to you."

She glared at me and subsided. I said, "Besides, we wouldn't want anything to happen to this purse, Megan. Considering what it contains."

I sprung the little clasp and the purse popped open. Lying there among her compact, lipstick and handkerchief were the pearls. I lifted them out and held them toward the sun. They seemed to absorb the sunlight, bloom and grow more radiant. They looked like molten gold. Too hot to handle. "The famous pearls," I said at last and dropped them in my pocket. "For days everyone's been asking me what I was getting out of the case. Finally it comes down to this, Megan: I get the pearls."

Her face was as hard and as cold as bronze. "Give them to me," she grated. "They're mine."

"Now that Alejandro's dead, now that Anita's dead, I agree. They're yours now."

"But you have them. Please give them back."

"Just like that," I said wonderingly. "Give them back. Your sister's dead because of these pearls. She's dead because you took them and hid them and a man thought she'd done that when it was you. I think you went downstairs as soon as the shot was fired and opened the safe and took the pearls. You left the safe open to make it look like robbery. That was clever. But it would have been cleverer to close the safe again and lock it. Only your nerve failed you or you were confused because things were happening too fast. You'd had the combination a long time because Molly gave it to you. She told me so last night. And all along I thought you'd gotten it somehow from Alejandro one early morning in bed."

Her gloved hand stabbed out and slapped across my mouth. A smear of blood blotted into the soft whiteness. My tongue tasted salty wetness. I licked my lip. Only a little cut. I dabbed at my lip with my handkerchief and said, "All right. The point is you had the combination, saw your chance and stole the pearls. They still didn't belong to you with Alejandro dead. They belonged to Anita. But you stole them from her and she was killed."

I spat on the water. A little blob of bloody foam. The current whirled it away.

"We'll go back now," I said.

"And the pearls?"

I leaned over and drew the dory alongside. "Get in. We'll talk about the pearls on the way back."

Sullenly she stepped over the side. I made no move to help her. One high heel stuck in the duckboards, she balanced awkwardly and gave a little cry. I said, "Don't let little things upset you. Big things don't."

Then I got into the dory, cast off and bent to the oars.

As we neared the dock, I said, "The pearls are yours, Megan. By right of inheritance and as partial payment for the Baron's wrongs. There's no one left to contest them because Garaldo's gone too. Garaldo would have paid me a good price for them but I saved them for you, the rightful owner—by law of elimination."

Her small white teeth had bitten deep into her lower lip but she would be able to stand the pain. That and anything else.

I said, "I think you precipitated old Lucia's murder by trying to blackmail the pearls from Alejandro as soon as you learned Garaldo had come here. But Alejandro took direct measures and eliminated Lucia as a threat. You didn't tell the police about Garaldo because there was always a chance Alejandro's murder could be pinned on Anita, as an accessory at least. That would have done away with the final legal obstacle to the pearls; but things didn't work out that way and Macaluso wrung your sister's neck. To you it added up to the same thing. Anita out of the way."

The boat bumped against the dock and I laid off the oars. She sat on the thwart staring at me, her face as immobile as granite. I tossed the mooring line through a ring and secured the dory. She didn't get up and climb out, she still sat there. Still waiting.

I said, "You hid the pearls on my boat yesterday. It was a safe place because it was an unlikely place. But a place you could always return to. With or without me. When you did that you weren't the little lost girl, despoiled and wronged by a satyr. Not anymore. Not any longer. That made you a thief. With your sister's blood on you."

I fished for the pearls and lifted them into the sunlight again. "Take a long look, Megan, because the next time you'll see them will be in the office of the insurance company. They're going to be found today. Not by me—by the police. For charity. The only charitable act you'll be part of the rest of your life."

She stood up and stepped stiffly out onto the dock.

"Is that all?" she said icily.

"I guess so," I said and fought a thick lump in my throat. "Words …" I said and then my voice trailed away.

She turned and ran up the landing stairs, her heels making little sharp clicks on the varnished wood. A young lady with her future ahead of her. A big future. As big as the whole outdoors.

I got out of the dory wearily and pulled myself up the steps. When I got to the top I could see her getting into a cab. The meter flag popped up and the cab growled away in a cloud of smoke.

I felt sick and disillusioned, but that was nothing new. That was the least of it. I thought about Megan. There would be lovers and a series of husbands and unfaithfulness and decadence and finally old age. The scene flashed before my eyes like dissolves from a newsreel. The pearls. In my pocket they were as heavy as anchor chain.

I trudged slowly up to the clubhouse, went into the bar and climbed up on a stool. The bartender poured three fingers of scotch and I gulped it like iced tea. It made me feel better, but not much.

After that I pulled over the telephone and called Kellaway.

THE END

Manufactured by Amazon.ca
Acheson, AB

12814937R00090